If I'm one in a million, that means there are
at least seven of me here in Washington State alone.
Find me, my brothers and sisters in battle,
let us show them why they are right
to fear our power.

REDEMPTION THROUGH RETRIBUTION IN THE GREY CENTURY OF ANTI-REVOLUTION

GREGOR FJELLREV

BLUE FORGE PRESS
Port Orchard, Washington

Blue Forge Press is the print division of the volunteer-run, federal 501(c)3 nonprofit company, Blue Legacy, founded in 1989 and dedicated to bringing light to the shadows and voice to the silence. We strive to empower storytellers across all walks of life with our four divisions: Blue Forge Press, Blue Forge Films, Blue Forge Gaming, and Blue Forge Records. Find out more at: www.MyBlueLegacy.org

Blue Forge Press
7419 Ebbert Drive Southeast
Port Orchard, Washington 98367
blueforgepress@gmail.com
360-550-2071 ph.txt

Table of Contents

One Frame 9

Spheres of Annihilation 19

MacGuffinite 29

Slice the Wind 41

Avenger, Thyself Avenge 51

The Planet of Time 61

Merciful Morons Need Not Apply 71

I Will Walk the Shadowed Path 81

Retribution Done Right Defies the Cycle 89

I Beheld Red Sparks 99

May Flame Await the Luck-Blessed 109

Solace Only in Solitude 119

An Ode to the Augment 129

An Interview with Gregor Fjellrev 143

REDEMPTION THROUGH RETRIBUTION IN THE GREY CITY OF ANTI—REVOLUTION

GREGOR FJELLREV

ONE FRAME

That was when I realized what I had done. I didn't even know I had this power, until it was unconsciously called upon in my time of need. I looked at my attacker, his frozen expression seemed to be an attempt at furious contempt, though I wouldn't call it fury, since it was about the same kind of fire that ignites a toddler's temper tantrums. The knife he had just tried to stick me with hovered inches away from my torso. I took a step back, eyeing the scene, this screenshot in time itself. I didn't know how I did it, or how to reverse it, so I didn't want to make assumptions just yet. I tentatively reached towards his arm and grabbed the weapon from it, everything still frozen and inert. After wriggling the knife free from his right hand, I took a look at the label on it. A Benchmade. It'd fetch a reasonable price at a pawn shop, considering their typical triple-digit retail value.

But now was the issue of this little man who tried to stab me. I could just tell that there was nothing to this person but the kind of screeching brattiness that even drove him to attempt to attack me. For the apparently capital crime of not bending knee to his will, he intended me dead. My curiosity in the limits of my newfound power got the better of me as I dragged the blade across his throat while time was standing still. No blood fell from the wound, there was only a gash in the static flesh, only a crimson pillar of sliced muscle, artery and vein alike behind it, ready to start bleeding once I permitted time its course again.

Ten more steps away, outside of the alley he had lured me in to, and I consciously thought to myself, 'Time may resume now.'

And so it did. I ducked away as the corner of my eye saw him drop to his knees, unable to breathe, let alone speak in the wake of my strike. I felt no remorse. After all, if such trivial matters as his quarrel were worth killing over, they were worth his dying over, as far as I was concerned.

I cleaned the knife off before taking it in to sell. The only news the following day was that a known mugger and purse-snatcher was found dead in an alleyway, his throat split open seemingly by a mark who proved that this trash bit off more than he could chew. That meant that I would see no repercussions as long as I told no one of the incident, and I would tell no one. That's the advantage of working alone; you know everyone, and whether or not they'll rat you out. And unless you've got a few screws loose in your head, you won't rat yourself out.

So what next? I wondered. I had this power, and I would be damned before I used it responsibly. Or rather, by a very pretentious person's definition of 'responsibility,' as in, not at all.

I needed to know more about this power of mine. What were its limits? Could it last only for a few minutes or could I pause the world indefinitely? What was its scale? Was it simply freezing time in an area, or was all of time itself truly frozen for however long? What nuances might there be in activating and deactivating it? I sure didn't want to accidentally resume time while inside a bank vault or governor's mansion. I needed to test this, figure it out. I couldn't risk anything less.

In time, I came to understand what I was capable of. There seemed to be no upper limit to how long I could pause time. And it was a true freeze-frame of time, not just myself being accelerated in speed to such a degree that everything else seemed to pause. Otherwise, simply tapping on some glass while the power was active would shatter it. That's how I figured that part out. To my surprise, I also discovered that there was no caveat to resuming time, I had to will it specifically. I couldn't 'accidentally' start time again, as I had initially worried.

The scope of my power seemed more immense than reality itself would permit. I searched very hard for the obnoxious downside, but could not find it. I suppose the downside would be that if I were killed during such a pause, time may remain frozen forever as its key-holder would no longer be alive to unlock it.

Even with all this knowledge and understanding of what I was capable of, I knew I had to use it in a way that did not allow its discovery. What I would do needed to at least be *possible* by mortal means, so I couldn't just poke a dozen holes in some billionaire as he walked along the promenade, lest the nature of power, even if not mine specifically be divulged.

But I could poke a dozen holes in them during the night, in that infinitesimal split second between moments in time that would ensure my non-detection. But even then, I had to leave no trace behind. I know what forensic power is ready to be brought to bear to unmask an assassin who does favors for the world, I know what wretched skill is ready to find out who liberated the people from a great and heavy boot on their necks. *How did he do it?* they would ask. It wouldn't matter if they could prove that I, at the very least, did do it.

And so I began my planning. What funds I would need came from what I'd take from the kinds of people no one rational would want to aid. Whenever I drove about town, I'd see some house with a black and white version of the American flag with a single blue stripe, or some other regalia of fascism, and then I would pause time, walk in undetected and clean them out of their valuables. I had a pair of gloves and a separate pair of shoes from what I normally wore, to swap out with before beginning. In the back of my car, a dark blue morph suit ensured that stray hairs and dead skin wouldn't be left behind. Even if the material was, it wasn't DNA. Dark blue because that's what I had. I originally got it years ago, because the color of night is dark blue, not black. Makes for the best camouflage when the sun is down.

Even then, it was honestly more preparation than necessary to make even the poutiest local sheriffs give up bothering. But I suppose it's better to have it and not need it, than vice versa. It was an extra layer of insurance that guaranteed success through non-failure.

To move the stolen goods, I'd often just extract the stones and melt down the metals of jewelry, to then sell them to a mint office for a bit under the spot price for not being assayed. Whatever. Not like I paid for the metal anyways. I did make sure never to say that, though. I had a plethora of excuses and answers ready for questions, but to my surprise, nobody ever asked.

Cash was cash from the houses of these assholes, and coins were sold to shops as long as they were silver and not gold. You could walk into a place with five hundred silver eagles and no one would bat an eye. So much as twenty gold eagles, and people start asking questions. I often even left those gold coins in the houses, having also taken pretty much the rest of their life's savings, to add a little twist of the knife, that they'd have to sell that precious round. I always enjoyed imagining the frustration they would have as they sold off the one remaining thing of value they had left, to an unflinching negotiator giving them scraps for it, out of knowledge of their desperation. It was the deserved fate of every one of these despicable people I thrust it upon. I never, *never* steal from people who are of sound morals.

So like I said, my targets were relegated to those other types, you know the lot. Whether their excessive piety was made clear with Bible-verse bumper stickers, Confederacy regalia, or a full-on fucking swastika in their windows. And I don't mean the actual Hindu version, but I think that's kind of obvious at this point.

Even as I kept doing this, making more money than I needed to, to live comfortably, I had to remember what I was planning. The first big one. A spree of targeted heists on suburban blights there may have been in the news, but there were no leads, no suspects. I hardly cared as long as that was the case, given my power to pause time and therefore, take it.

Eventually, something floated into the harbor that angered me so much, I changed my plans on the spot. The abomination was massive, a floating mansion that served as exemplar to everything that's wrong with the world. Oh yes, it was one of *those* yachts.

Normally, I would've simply planned to clean it out a bit, grab the expensive bottles and golden tableware, but when I saw that egregious vessel, seemingly draining the very color of the world around it... when I saw the dozens of overly armed guards, all with their stupid fancy rifles, vests and sidearms, I knew; I couldn't just settle for anything less.

I froze time again, halting all things in their place. I had planned to kill only the owner. But when I looked again upon the veritable army that was on the boat, the ostentatious guests aboard the insufferably luxurious vessel, I knew I couldn't just stop at one. Not for something like this. Not for such a beacon of evil that dared float in that harbor.

Time stood still as I boarded the craft, looking for the armory that equipped all these pigs with their obscene weapons and armors. When I found it, I was lucky to see that someone was accessing it at the time, and the door was consequently open in this frozen point. I grabbed what I wanted, and I laced the entire fucking boat with it. There would hardly be anything left of the thing once I set this chain reaction off.

And hardly anything left there sure was.

In my zeal, I hadn't even considered the consequences of my blatancy in action. The black boxes and what security camera footage could be salvaged showed one instant, nothing wrong, while the next instant saw the entire yacht rigged to blow.

The story was breaking news for a whole month, where I also learned why they even had so many explosives on board: Apparently, the billionaire owner of the vessel had them specifically to destroy the boat 'just in case the peasant revolt was about to claim it.' Dude literally was planning to pull a Scorched Earth with his boat if it came down to it. I was glad to use that against him. Well, what was left of him anyway. He was on board when it went up in a great and glorious ball of fire.

And so the confusion as to how it happened began as assuredly as it would. How did the explosives get there in one instant to another? Some suspected that the cameras were blinded somehow, but even if that were the case, how did it all get rigged up without someone noticing? I paid it no mind, honestly. I am willing to allow it to become one of the great historical mysteries, that would only be solved centuries later once powers like mine became more common knowledge. That there were 'classical' examples of people like me, hidden among the rest of the population. I don't know. Not like I'd live long enough to see it anyway. Not like I care.

In the aftermath of this, my boldest endeavor yet, I decided to lay low until the heat calmed down, only using my abilities in an opportunistic way. If I saw someone I knew to be wealthy, I would relieve him of his wallet's cash quickly. If I saw someone else being accosted or assaulted, I would remove the threat discreetly, and chalk up my sudden appearance to the tunnel vision of everyone else involved. My awareness of my need to use my power tactfully would ensure that it was done as such.

But everything changed when I saw something that I figured should have been impossible. As I sorted through the bills of another suited man's wallet, who wouldn't miss a few hundred, probably would even figure he just forgot to put cash in it that day, I saw someone moving through the frozen crowd. Someone who was not affected by my ability to stop time.

Slipping the wallet back into the pocket of this well-off prick, I approached the person in movement, discovering only then that they seemed to be looking for me.

"There you are," he said. "Took me long enough, eh?"

Once I resumed time again, and everyone resumed their normal course, this man and I agreed to discuss things over a light lunch at a nearby cafe. I offered to pay for us both, considering the donation recently made by no one of consequence.

"I can't do what you're doing, myself," he explained. "But I seem to be immune to the effect."

"You figured it out yourself, then?" I asked.

"Yeah, I realized pretty quickly that I wasn't controlling the time stops, only immune to them. So I wasn't gonna chance it with... well, basically what you're doing."

"So how did you find me?"

"That's the other thing. Every time you've done it, I've had this... *sense* of in which direction the stop was originating. Never an exact location, but whenever time was stopped, I could just *tell* from which direction its origin point was in relation to me. I've just followed since. I suspect you were testing the limits of your power for a while, considering the uh... the..." He tried to find his next words, then took a moment to think of them. It was obvious he knew what he wanted to say, all that was left was to figure out how to say it. "...the density of temporal pause events earlier on. It seemed congruent with a sort of 'testing the limits' period. I mean, it's exactly what I would've done."

I nodded to let him know he made sense. "And here I thought that I was about to find the caveat."

The man across from me laughed. "I know *exactly*

what you mean! Yeah. You get the power to freeze time at will but someone out there is immune and is constantly trying to kill you whenever you do it. That sort of thing?"

I nodded again.

"Well, here I was, worried that the person doing it would turn out to be an asshole. Looks like you're just doing favors for the world."

He then nodded to me knowingly, and I paused time for everyone but us again, to ensure the privacy of what he was about to say next.

"I assume the yacht job was you?"

I nodded.

"Nice."

Time resumed once more.

"I always did say that if I'm one in a million, that means there's at least six of me here in Washington State alone. And if we found each other, people would be right to fear our power."

I nodded as I understood what he was saying. It was obvious what to do next. Indeed, two ones in a million had found each other, and the enemies of honor would be right to fear our combined power.

Sure, we won't be the ones to save the world, but perhaps we can at least get the ball rolling.

Spheres of Annihilation

That," I summarized, "is about the single most dangerous trap you can come across in your entire career as a dungeoneer!"

My lecture was to be on the first of Fall. I hadn't planned it within the month itself, but apparently the local Harvest God's month started on the day I was meant to give this lecture to a bunch of Adventurer's Academy hopefuls.

They had potential, as far as I was aware, but I hadn't yet figured out who everybody was. Between the archetypes of the goody two-shoes who thinks he's hot shit; the lurkers in the back row who were only here because their parents paid for the rent in student housing; the ones who actually wanted to become adventurers and see the world, and the ones who just shouldn't be here because they clearly already have the knowledge? I had only figured out the first of those demographics.

A pity, too, because I *hate* those types. You know the sorts, the ones diligently taking notes in neat formatting and styles and being a Type A Rules Lawyer (Type A ones being the 'by-the-book' brats who snitch and tattle on even the most minor of infractions, while Type B Rules Lawyers use the rules to as exacting a definition as they can so they can get away with as much as possible) and thinking that they're earning the teacher's favor by being that kind of person. If not for the fact they'd probably report me to the administration, I'd kick them out of the class first thing. Believe me, many academics sigh with relief whenever *those* types are absent. Unfortunately, perfect attendance is in their nature, and the best I could do was groan alongside the students whenever they asked about homework.

I remember I was one of the ones throwing my bookbags at them when I was in those seats. But I digress.

I was lecturing about Spheres of Annihilation, as this was the unit about traps in dungeons. Last week was Dwarven IEDs and Kobold Swarm Deployers. Easiest way out of the latter is to toss a copper bar down the corridor as a distraction. Works every time.

"A Sphere of Annihilation is *not* to be confused with an Orb of Nothing, by the way!" I pointed out, for its truthfulness. "Between the two, one is devilishly tricky to summon, stabilize *and* bind, while the other is a solipsistic facsimile that isn't *as* bad, but I mean... whenever I came across either in a dungeon, I just walked out and went to a different one! There's plenty of places to scour within the ruins of Algarith-Zaxhilim that'll pay for a night's worth of room and board...."

I stopped myself before I trailed off. "But I digress," I corrected. "This is the Advanced Dungeoneering class, not Beginning. You all do understand the difference between Aetherial and Primordial schools of sorcery?"

Everyone either nodded or put their hands up, ready to define the difference between these two sources of power. It at least indicated to me that I could continue in my definitions of a Sphere of Annihilation trap.

"A Sphere of Annihilation is typically the last line of defense immediately before a mage-tower's Main Vault, not to mention the ultimate show of force of an Aethermage's mastery." I continued: "They're usually right in front of the door mechanism itself, whether it's visible or camouflaged. It's what distinguishes the vault of a casual Magi from an Archmage's Artifact Repository."

As soon as I said 'artifact,' I saw several ears perk up from the Dragonkin in the crowd.

"While most Mage Tower vaults simply contain quantities of gold, silver, gems, and other precious metals, an Archmage's Artifact Repository contains a wealth of potently enchanted magical items. Things that will fetch a minimum of four digits worth of gold pieces at your typical city's Artificer or Enchanter shop. And they are almost as tricky to disperse as they are to summon. If the dungeon you're in is decently populated, you can actually sort of 'cheat' the process by just throwing your enemies into it until the thing runs out of charges and disperses itself. This usually takes about twenty enemies thrown, so finding a nearby bandit camp to infiltrate and lure people from should not be discarded as an option."

Several students furiously scribbled down notes, particularly the fact that one didn't actually *have* do disarm a Sphere of Annihilation trap.

"Now then, if all else fails, and you still *really* want to get past that Sphere, here's what you do to disarm it...."

My explanation, fortunately, was not lost on these ears. Eventually, the gong signaled the end of the period and no further reason for anyone to be in the room.

"Professor Akidor?" One of the students came up to

my desk as the rest funneled out. I sat up, ready to hear his question. "I managed to get basically everything else noted, but one of the steps you mentioned for the Sphere of Annihilation trap seemed really confusing...."

"Which one?" I asked in return.

"Well, on the manual disarm, you mentioned a Phase Interval Window of about two seconds after successfully disrupting the Binding Runes. Now then, I know that means one has two seconds to actually produce a Metastable Current Flow before the thing just detonates, but I don't think any of us were actually taught *what* a Phase Interval Window is, specifically."

I raised an eyebrow. "You mean to tell me that someone else neglected to define Phase Interval Windows?"

He nodded, but hesitantly, as though that weren't the correct answer, even though it was true.

"The hell's wrong with some of my colleagues?" I cursed towards the nameless colleague who didn't prepare these students adequately. As much as I didn't care how they used this knowledge, I cared that they gained it. They were here by choice, and they should be getting their time's worth, damn it. "A Phase Interval Window is the time between a particularly volatile arcane phenomenon's stable and unstable states. When you destabilize something like a Sphere of Annihilation, after about two seconds, that destabilization manifests in the form of flattening the building it's in, or producing a great crater in place of a dungeon if it's underground. It's like the time between putting the wrong reagent into an alembic, and the thing shattering from the reaction."

He nodded with an 'ah,' and the purple spectral cat on

his shoulder quickly jotted down what I had said into his diary. Most professors hate it when you use Familiars to take notes for you, but I don't mind it at all. If it works for you, then it works, as far as I'm concerned. Only pretentious twats actually insist on a particular 'style' of note-taking within their classes, let alone to the point of making it an actual matter of grade. The nerve of those guys, who've got no business calling themselves academics, let me tell you. No, don't let me tell you, on second thought. That would be a *massive* tangent that I could go on for *days* about, and frankly, nobody needs to hear that particular rant.

Regardless, I had answered the Dragonkin's question, and that was good enough for now. Once he exited, I sat there, moving a small orb of flame between my fingers as I consulted my Pondering Orb. There was something on my mind indeed, and it wasn't even Spheres of Annihilation. Though admittedly, they are fascinating in their construction, not least of all for how much effort is required to construct them properly. Someone has to value whatever lies behind that door so much that they undergo such a dangerous, not to mention far from cheap, arcane process. Further still, one must value finding out what lies behind said door to an even higher degree to be willing to bother getting past such a time and resource intensive trap that is as effective as it is a hassle to summon and bind, let alone properly.

I eyed the pouch of Summoning Circle Dust on my desk. I considered a live demonstration on the morrow, to see if there was one among my class with some real proper potential. I had barely yet figured out who all the players were, where all of the archetypes of students were represented. Of course, putting an emergency kill switch on any trap is properly annoying, but I was sure willing to go that extra step in the name of safety. Hell, I'd just send the bill to the requisitions department at the academy. If they don't pay it, they'll have to contend with someone who is capable of summoning a Sphere of Annihilation. Either way, no skin off my back.

The next day rolled around, and the students walked in to see that hovering black orb of pure darkness in the center of the room, above my summoning circle. Several of them were shocked; one student ran out of the room. I chuckled because that person specifically was one of the goody two-shoes snitch-tattletale hybrids and harbingers of misery and frustration that I had previously identified. A few others saw that the binding circle had Killswitch Runes in it, so they knew I was in control of this thing.

"Today is a day for practical demonstration," I said. "One of you who is still here is going to be able to disarm this thing; all that I have yet to do is find out which among you can knock over a Sphere of Annihilation."

I heard a few comments from the crowd:

"Is he nuts?!"

"There's Killswitch Runes, it couldn't go wrong if it wanted to."

Even a casual:

"Well, that's definitely one way to test us."

The sphere hovered ominously.

Another Human stepped out of the hall, just in case things went wrong.

The sphere continued to hover ominously.

Two Dragonkin looked at it curiously, but dared not

touch it.

So far, so good, I thought. Now we knew who everybody was. I recognized one of the Dragonkin from yesterday, the one who asked for a clearer definition of a Phase Interval Window.

"Well, I know for a fact this sphere at least has an emergency kill-switch Dispel...." the Dragonkin said as he examined the circle. "Though it would seem to be nonfunctional, because this rune is wrong... no, it isn't! It's just an *Elder* Version of the rune, which is stronger than the Standard Version of these runes. Devil's in the details on this one."

"So far, so correct," I answered then nodded, motioning for him to continue analyzing it.

"Well, it actually looks like an Energetic Overload could cancel it out and force a dispersion."

I nodded to him to go ahead and try it. He pulled his hands back and began conjuring an orb of raw arcane power. It grew in his hands, pulsating as it grew in potency, crackling with golden arcs of lightning around its edges.

He held the thunderous orb in his hands for a moment, still eyeing the Sphere and calculating whether or not he had enough power summoned to disperse it. It was like he was holding his breath for as long as he could, squeezing out what more Mana could be pumped into this sphere of electromagical current. At the last possible second, he flung it forward and it went into the Sphere, causing it to pulsate and destabilize, crunching and collapsing upon itself as it could not handle the sheer sudden input of raw power it experienced. The Sphere vanished in a gust of wind, dispersing the glowing pink circle of what was the Summoning Circle Dust that bound the Sphere to the physical realm.

"I think that works," he then said, and I nodded, impressed. The applause from several other students could be heard as this test had been passed with flying colors.

"Most clever work," I noted. "A single maneuver that both detonated the Sphere but also dispersed the Circle! What explosive force would have been unleashed was simply stopped dead by the breaking of the circle, and the energy simply canceled out."

"That's the method, aye."

"Seems we all are learning new things here," I commented. This was a method that had not been tested yet for Spheres of Annihilation. Energetic Overloads work on a majority of arcane traps, but it had generally been accepted that a Sphere of Annihilation was simply too complex for such a basic method to work. And for a while, it was. But nobody had considered precision *alongside* magnitude for that technique. An absolutely sensible approach, but it seemed nobody had gotten around to attempting it.

But it worked. A new method of disarming Spheres of Annihilation had been found. How often it would be called upon, however, was likely not too common, considering how rarely in actuality these spheres pop up. Like I had said the previous day, typically only in the personal Vault Towers of Archmagi would you find even a single Sphere.

With one promising prospect identified, and many others clearly taking notes, I decided the next lesson was going to be a bit easier. Hell, if these guys can get past a Sphere of Annihilation intact, there probably isn't much they can't conquer. Naturally, next week is going to be how to deal with Acidic Rhinezone generators.

Of course, as I consulted the Pondering Orb after the class period was over, I found myself wondering why I ached so terribly to perform that practical demonstration. The question was answered almost as quickly as it had been worded in my mind, however. The kind of person I am... is not particularly conducive to university desk work. Much as the teaching position paid well—*as it should,* my very thoughts emphasized—it is still the case that I am quite incurably a Dungeoneer, seeking eternally the thrill of making it past a door that nobody else had conquered since it had been sealed.

Then again, I certainly had identified a promising candidate for an apprentice....

MacGuffinite

The three of us stood there, revolvers in each hand pointed at each other. A classic standoff, whose novelty wouldn't be lost if it weren't for the sheer frivolousness of the matter. All of our hands were unflinching, for better or for worse. Whether it was good that our aim knew no falter, and such did our resolve, or condemnable that we were so ready and prepared to end each other's lives is a question well beyond my pay-grade.

"It's not what we thought it was, let's start there." I finally broke the silence. "Nobody has to lower their guns yet, but let's start with that fact. It's not what we thought it was."

The two men who had somehow arrived at this cavern at the same time as myself nodded. Despite that agreement, cold steel barrels still pointed at everyone's faces, at least a pair of them. Our fingers were still away from the triggers, held at their side as we knew that wrapping that pointer around them would illicit fiery response. We were all trained well enough to watch for it. We all had been through enough firefights to know how they work, and how to win them. Three very skilled men, ready for hell to break loose in an instant. That was us as our gazes alternated between each other, and the object of our fixation on the pedestal between us.

"Were we all told different things?" the man on my left asked of us all, himself included. "I was told it was a construction tool, meant to build cities and repair ruins, the chance to make the world better by way of fixing it."

"They told me it was a weapon," the man on my right answered. "That it was capable of razing those cities to the ground, the chance to make the world better by ridding it of its enemies and ruining their enclaves and strongholds."

It was now my turn to answer. "What I heard was that whatever it was, it couldn't stay in this world. Whether because it could build or destroy, it was too powerful and needed to be ridden of. The chance to make the world better by removing the catalyst for its end, whether by fire or by burying it alive with stone and steel."

"So there's one thing in common," Left responded. "We all were told it was a chance to make the world better. One way or another... better."

"Clearly we all try to be men of honor, then," I proposed. "How about we all show it?"

A few seconds later, six revolvers hit the stone floor of the cavern and we all breathed a sigh of relief. But we knew that those guns weren't the only weapons we had. Whether ankle holsters or knives or our gods-given hands and feet, we were all far from disarmed. But the immediate threat was over, and now we weren't a hair-twitch away from our mutual destruction.

"All right," I began after we all took a breather. "What's next?"

"I'd rather not find out that one of us is a sneaky

opportunist, personally," Right confessed.

"If nothing else, we've made sure that we're still on even ground," Left pointed out. "We were a few seconds ago, we still are. That we're not an instantaneous decision away from death is an added bonus."

"Point taken."

I rolled my shoulders, staring at the thing that made us all ready to kill each other, and arguably still was actively working at it. I needed to piece my next words together in my head before I let them out of my mouth, and I bet the other two were thinking the exact same thing of themselves. Nobody wanted to make a misstep. Whether because we all wanted to be on the winning side of this encounter, or because we had our own motives to fulfill, death would put quite a damper on such plans all the same.

"Do we all agree that we want the same thing, that being to do the right thing?" I asked.

"Aye."

"Yep."

"Can we all agree to not pick up those guns from the floor until either we all walk out of here as friends, or only one of us does?"

"Aye."

"Works for me."

"Okay, then." I sighed with relief, again. Progress was progress, and we all seemed to silently agree that we were making it. "Let's figure this out.... Were we all sent by the same concerned party, or who asked us to retrieve this thing?"

"I was approached by a concerned political party leader," Right began. "He expressed a deep worry that what he called a weapon could fall into some nondescript enemy's hands, and that it should be secured by someone else first."

"Don't tell me a politician actually tried to convince you he was more trustworthy to have such a weapon!" Left scoffed, to which Right chuckled as he sat down on a nearby rock.

"No," Right answered. "He didn't try to convince me of anything. He just mentioned how bad it would be if it fell into the wrong hands, and that I should go and grab the thing. Very much silently suggesting that I return it to him, or at the very least keep it for myself for him to call upon me to use it if the time should arise."

"He probably knew you wouldn't have any of it if he said it himself," I mentioned. Right nodded. "At the very least he knows you're not an idiot."

"Though I was told the opposite, I was told by a banker type," Left explained himself. "A guy who had enough money to build such a city on his own damn self, but would definitely rather someone else did it for him. Or in this case, something else like a city-building MacGuffin like this."

"Building things costs money," Right pointed out. "Anyone who has more than they'll ever need doesn't want to spend a penny of it, because that'd be too beneficial to people who aren't themselves."

Both Left and myself nodded vigorously in agreement, before Left continued: "No kidding. Same as you, though, he never directly suggested I give it to him. Just retrieve it and hang onto it until a time of need."

My turn again. "I was told by a priest that this thing had to be destroyed. I'm far from a religious man myself, but I can understand a need to keep absolute power absolutely out of anyone's hands."

Left paced around the room as Right sat on his rock, myself leaning against the stone wall of the cavern. "What we have yet to do is figure out which one of those claims is correct," Left then said as he paced and eyed the thing. "Whether all or none, we still haven't seen for ourselves just what this thing does, or even if it does anything. For all we know we've been sent here to get into a standoff and subsequent shootout with each other."

"All three of them in cahoots just to get a few fighters killed?" Right asked. "That seems a bit far-fetched, even for those types."

"We're all very good at what we do, among the best," I mentioned. "It's not outside the realm of possibility that we've been sent to end up eliminating each other, thus removing a very real threat to all three establishments of power."

"If that *is* the case, then I say we blow this cavern and bury the thing, then take the fight to them," Left advocated. "If it turns out this thing can be used honorably, we can recover it later, or agree not to bother to."

The decision had been made. We numbered three as we walked outside the cavern chamber, our guns back in their holsters, and our leather jackets fluttering in the wind dramatically as our feet walked back towards the city. Left and Right stood at my sides, and myself in the middle, the ominous grey walls loomed before us in due time. As we walked those miles, we figured that now was the time to learn each other's names, since we would be brothers in cold steel and hot lead soon enough.

"I've got the city's speakers," Argus, formerly Left, noted as he pulled the hacking device from his pocket, accessing the network of speakers through this dystopia, that projected propaganda and silencing words of sweet comfort to the masses. "How about some mood music?"

"Start with *Resist and Bite,*" Sykar, the man on my right, suggested. "After that, leave it on shuffle. If you've got at least *that* song, I think we can trust the rest of your playlist."

"Of course I have *Resist and Bite,*" Argus scoffed. "Any self-respecting one-man army has *Resist and Bite* on their playlist."

"And any self-respecting one-woman army has *Night Witches,*" I heard a voice from behind us as we turned around.

"Son of a bitch, you're still alive!" I was stunned.

"Do I really look like the kind of person who dies? Come on, Talon! There were only eighty of them during that incident!" the Night Witch commented as she walked up to us.

The intro to the titular ballad began to play over the speakers Argus had hacked and we four turned back to face the enemy army that had gathered in the wake of our presence and obvious alliance.

We wasted no time laying waste to the scum that were the pawns of our employers. They chose their side, and so they had chosen death in their ignorance and unwillingness to do what was right. Whether out of fear or loyalty, death awaited them all the same as they deserve.

Within ten minutes, our trained flurries of lead and reloads had broken their ranks and scattered the pigs, and even behind their black armors and grey faceplates, the stench of fear was thick in the air… their fear of us, and what we represented.

"Argus, Talon, get the top floor office of that skyscraper! Our mutual employers are hiding there!" Sykar called out. "I and the Night Witch shall deal with the rest of the *Sturmtruppen!*"

"Fight well!" I yelled out as Argus and I began to make our way to the tower of steel, concrete and glass that did gash the sky with its dullard presence and draining, uninspired architecture that was the quintessence of the grey regime. As Argus and I entered the tower, we heard the cackling of the Night Witch as she entered glorious battle against the defenders of evil alongside Sykar, which told the two of us we could leave the streets in their hands.

Two guards stood before us in the lobby, drawing their weapons and ordering us to stand down. But we were quicker on the draw, and a hole in each of their chests secured our passage to the elevator and stairs.

I quickly called all of the elevators down to the ground floor as Argus figured out my plan. We told each of the elevators to climb to the topmost floor, one floor at a time, but stepped out as soon as the buttons had been pressed. We would have to race against the slow-climbing steel cages on the stairs, hoping that we could at least not be too far behind.

"Grapplers!" I called out as Argus and I both grabbed our respective traversal method from our belts, and made our own elevators in the stairwell, climbing five floors at a time far faster than our feet would have carried us.

With the elevators taking one floor at a time to get to

the top, we managed to keep pace. The automatic weapons fire that permeated the air behind the stairwell doors told us that the guards had fallen for our trick. As soon as we heard magazines hitting the floor, we burst through the stairwell door, weapons blazing in glory as the enemies of honor fell before us. Every hour of training we had ever undergone, that we had ever put ourselves through, it was on display here, and it was glorious.

A symphony of steel and lead cut down our foes before any of them could load new bullets into their guns. The flavor of the air around our enemies shifted from confusion, to fear, to panic as they realized that we were the walking incarnations of their destruction, of righteous retribution.

Taking an access card from the body of a dead guard, I opened the door to where the suits were cowering. Argus held his weapons high at them, ordering them not to move. One made a break for it, and was met with a bullet through his leg, which Argus then proceeded to drive his boot down on and twist it constantly, still keeping his revolvers trained on the rest of the grey and black-suited fiends, killers of worlds. I proceeded to the window to look down at the streets below, and saw that Sykar and the Night Witch still were making excellent progress. There were some resistors alongside them, civilians who finally had gained either the stones to join the fight, or finally found their chance to.

"They're doing all right," I commented.

"Thanks, Talon," Argus added. We were both more or less on the same wavelength. Argus then stomped on the suit's leg to break his already wounded limb sideways. "Since he won't exactly be going anywhere...."

"One of you gets to die quickly, the rest we're going to do our best to give you the fates you deserve. You may decide amongst yourselves who will go painlessly," I informed the men with more money than some had numbers for. Their end was at long last at hand, and the world would breathe great sighs of relief upon each of their last breaths.

As soon as I noticed the priest who had sent me to find the device that almost had me killing two men who I'm glad are now my allies instead, I put a few bullets through the window, and grabbed him, punching him a few times in the face before throwing him through the weakened glass window, most satisfying defenestration.

Argus fired shots into each of the limbs of those who remained, to at the very least put them into a state of too much pain to run away. I drove my knife through the thigh of one such runner to stop him, and sliced both of his Achilles tendons to seal the deal in that regard. His left Femoral artery had been severed by my knife, so I knew I could leave him there to bleed out as he screamed from two slashed Achilles.

After we were finished with the wretches, we also took care to write down how each of them died, so that the people could at least take solace that we made it hurt like they deserved. As we finished penning the notes for the history books, I heard an elevator door ping. The Night Witch was on the other side.

"Where's Sykar?" I asked.

"He's still down there, leading the resistance. I wanted to make sure you guys got this done, and it looks like you have... impressively, too."

"Is this the guy I broke the leg sideways after shooting

it?" Argus asked me to confirm.

"No, that's him over there." I pointed to the otherwise indistinguishably mangled body in the corner. "See? Red tie was on that one. That one's wearing a blue tie, he's the guy you stabbed in the Sciatic Nerve and then on the top of the feet—"

"Oh, right, right. Yeah, then I dragged him around the room for a bit across the broken glass from when you threw that one guy through the window," Argus recalled.

"That guy almost landed on Sykar, by the way," the Night Witch informed.

"Shit, that would've been embarrassing," I commented to her nod and Argus's nod.

"It ended up working out, though," the Night Witch continued. "Sykar basically looked at the guy and yelled out to the crowd, 'That's our sign that the gods are with us!' and I saw one of the pigs actually pull his weapon on his friends because he knew his side was done for."

"Find him and make sure he never sees the sun again," I instructed. "We can't have infiltrators in the midst of what we build next."

Argus nodded.

"Already did," the Night Witch informed. "He's in chains right now; he will answer for his evils committed whilst being on *their* side. Believe me, you'll have no argument from me calling the whole 'I was bad but now I'm good' bullshit out for what it is. He will answer for what he's done. They all will."

"Excellent," I said. "Once we finish mopping this place up, what do you say we head to the next city over? It'll be like old times plus two additional pairs of hands. Assuming you and Sykar want to join us, Argus?"

"Aye," Argus said as he double-checked the writings we had put down detailing the demises of the tyrants. "Wouldn't have it any other way."

"As for the cave, and whatever that thing was…." I started. "Let's just put the latitude-longitude coordinates in our diaries and maybe check up on it every few years. We dynamited the entrance, but you never know."

The Night Witch nodded. "Sounds like we've got our plans, then."

Argus closed the guestbook-turned-chronicle-of-death and nodded. "All right. Let's get to work."

Slice the Wind

nd then, they struck their target. Did you think those were drops of water falling from a leaf within a picturesque *beyul* hidden away from the world? No, they were my knives traveling through the air and into the chest of one of my enemies, who would gladly bulldoze such a place and replace it with grey towers of concrete, glass and steel.

First they struck him in the chest, and then another into the head of the guy standing next to him. They stood no chance against me as the rest of them, confused, looked around for who had just taken them by surprise in this forest.

Descending from the tree, I landed between them all as they realized their enemy was among them. The curved swords returned to my hands, yanked from the corpses they were resting in by way of my mastery of the wind.

They all drew their swords, seemingly in unison, planning to attack all at once. Now I had to get to work.

The best way to fight many men is to keep them all in front of you so that none can sneak up from behind. Being backed into a corner isn't necessarily a bad thing, as a cornered rattlesnake is the most dangerous kind. When one's back is to the wall, none can sneak up on you.

But I wasn't fighting these foes in a city, I was fighting them in a forest, laying waste to them as they tried so desperately to crush me underfoot, for whatever ridiculous reason they had. Maybe they were told to. Maybe they hated what I stood for. Maybe they hated my very existence. It mattered not. They were my enemy, and I shall fight them as I would any other: To the end.

Soon, their fallen corpses would produce greener patches of grass on the forest floor than the grass that surrounded them. If only because of how corpses make good fertilizer, instead of a grander context of relieving the world of such wicked people.

I have long debated with myself as these clashes grow more frequent, as the fallen of morals come upon this sanctum to ruin it for the difference it represents, the danger it symbolizes to their rule of stone and lead.

Am I the last man of honor in an honorless world? Am I all that remains of a bygone era where skill is valued? Did that era ever exist? Is its prospect forever vanished in the wake of the Human Scourge? Does the answer even matter, if even such an answer exists?

All I know now is that these humans, they would bring fire and death upon my sanctum, this place where I trained and forged myself into who I am today, and I will be damned before they pave it over with stone and build towers of steel and glass that serve only to drain the very air and sky of its lifeblood. The only steel that will find itself a friend of mine is the steel my weapons are forged of, steel that slices through the wind before slicing the throats of my enemies.

Indeed, they fall before me as they always do. Admittedly, I do take the most valuable of their possessions from their husks. Not like they'll need them anymore. Besides, they started it, and attacked me and my home first. To the victor go the spoils. A reward for a job well done, that even my foes' tools and valuables will now aid my cause, the cause of... well, I'm not sure if I've even got one. All I know is that I do all in my power to walk an honorable path, and that's cause enough for me.

That path, it would seem, leads me out of this forest sanctuary, as it has become more clear than ever that what I once called sanctuary no longer is such. That path will lead me to their strongholds and their fortresses, their citadels of evil that no army can breach... for it is not an army that it takes to breach it.

The thing about such citadels and fortresses, is that it is not in their destruction and flattening where victory over them lies, but instead the depopulation of the thralls of evil that occupy them. But how to succeed in such a campaign? The answer is as simple as it is massively difficult to implement: Unleash one warrior. True as it is that one warrior is not an army, one warrior needs not fight an army to bring it low. One at a time, two if they can. Three if they can handle a crowd of that level, but when one is surrounded by enemies, it only means that they've locked themselves into an arena with someone like me. It only takes one decision to become that person, or begin the path to becoming them.

Or in this case, *me* specifically. And in this case, this specific citadel of theirs, where the thralls of evil make their home, I shall unleash myself upon, in the name of the glades like my own that allow those like myself to build the skill required to take the fight to them.

In the name of the sanctuaries, I shall bring doom

upon theirs.

In the name of the wind I have learned to so precisely slice, so shall I slice these grey legionnaires to ribbons with those same strikes, my sword cleaving through them with the same ease. My fire and zeal is as endless as my defiance and spite.

But it is not without cost. More pretentious types would say it casts a dark mark on my soul to deliver so much vengeance, but that is not the cost. It is not a cost at all to me, because I've spent so long training myself to do it right. No, the cost is the fact that with my tools as tailored and sharpened as the ones I wield, their maintaining is costly, even more so is their replacement, should they break under the stress of the battles I put them through, the evil that I have them vanquished. Though the effects and armaments of the dark troopers I vanquish act as my income, it is still incredibly annoying when I have to so frequently maintain and replace my gear. Not for the fact of its cost, but what it means. It means there are so many....

But I will not cease the sharpening of my blades against the flesh of evildoers. I will not cease cleaving through their organs and bones, though I grow weary of seeing so many death-deservers. It is not in the act of taking their lives that makes my heart heavy. It is simply that there are so many that must be taken, and they seem without number. Though I know that number is finite, I do not know what that number is. All I hope is that what I do is making some kind of difference, relieving the world of those who breathe a sigh of relief for every one of their last breaths.

My solace is found in that though I may tire, there may be someone out there who does not tire of knowing that I remain, despite popular demand. I know not who they are, nor where they are. I know not if even they know I exist, but in a world with so many humans upon it, I find it hard to believe I am the last man of honor, though it sure as hell feels like it.

Though I know not if there are others like me, let alone how to find them, I also know I don't have to. Though I am alone, I do not consider it misfortune. I don't despair over my lack of allies beyond cold steel. Though I know how painful it may sound to hear, whether for its mockable edge or the heart-burdening fact that this truly is my understanding of the world around me, but all I ask if I am granted permission to ask anything, is not to insult me with pity. Do not curse my life with the patronizing, insipid spittle of what fools would claim to be sage.

I need no pity nor confidence from others, nor do I seek the latter or wish the former, though I feel as though these words I use to occupy my mind's space seem only to pass the seconds as I carve through the enemies that stand before me, erasing pawns and knights of evil alike while clearing the board of the weapons of the commanders.

The keeping of a cult of evil is a nigh unfathomably intense lifetime investment. It takes all those years and all those funds to indoctrinate and keep in line, to prevent the cultists from piercing the lies. All those years and funds before they entrust a weapon to the hands of their thralls, and every kill is that many years and that many funds down the drain. Not even a kill; maiming or wounding still is that much time and money before they can resume their evil ways. A broken bone takes six weeks to mend at least, and if it's hands or feet, far longer to rehabilitate. Anything is something, anything at all, and it will add up in time. It only takes one decision to be the flick of the dominoes, one decision to not stand idle when evil is beheld.

The citadel I infiltrated my way into is now empty. It only takes one decision. I don't know what the next step is, all I know is that I'm moving forward, as forward in time as in space, and forward towards the next darkness to vanquish.

Citadel by citadel, brick by brick if I must make it a matter of bricks instead of citadels.

Another day, another bastion of evil falls before me. I can't tell if it feels the same or different this time, and I find myself having trouble remembering what glory feels like, or if I've even felt it at all.

It's also been quite a while since I left that sanctuary, but I know it remains secret. I would be able to tell if it had fallen, believe me.

"Brick by brick, too?"

The voice had spoken from behind me, but not in the shadows. I heard a thud and I turned to see the limp corpse of a fascist on the floor... and the person behind me who was cleaning off their sword with the coat of the fallen scum.

"Always," I replied as calmly as I could, though I'm not sure why I suddenly needed to order myself to be calm; I normally just am. Weird.

"Well, I'll keep going down this hall. The armory has also been wired to blow, so you don't need to worry about that," the stranger added.

"Got it." I just stood, still and collected on the outside. "You want the commander, or should I keep on my route towards him?"

"Keep going on your route, we'll meet at the commander's quarters."

I nodded as they sprinted off down the hallway, and I heard someone's head smack against the brickwork as grunts and slices continued.

I caught my breath and shook myself back to a looser, more fight-ready state then jogged down the hallway of my own route, my sword at the ready to vanquish more world-killers in glorious battle.

We converged on the door to the leader of this cell's quarters, the name on the door identifying him as 'Vice-Prophet.'

"Why are they always so... cultist?" I wondered aloud.

"Just makes it all the more glorious to eradicate, if you ask me." My apparently new battle companion pointed out. I nodded, in a 'point taken' manner.

Remaining against the outside wall so any crossfire spray wouldn't hit us, I pushed the door open. Once the firing stopped, the silence that followed seemed to focus itself into a blade-like sharpness that allowed us to hear when the first magazine dropped from its rifle and hit the floor as the forces of darkness scrambled to reload. That's when we made our move.

We charged forward, eyes locked onto our targets as we drew back our swords simultaneously and drove them into the first enemy we reached. We worked our way from the outside in, cutting them down one by one in instants in time that seemed elongated in their sheer intensity. With every moment so vital, those moments seemed to slow down for the both of us, like our skill was such that the universe itself had no choice but to make sure that today, we would have our victory.

Their commander couldn't grab the pistol out of its holster fast enough as he realized we would soon be upon him. My blade disarmed him, quite literally. At the elbow. As for this mysterious warrior who was fighting beside me today, their sword went into and through his thigh, pinning him to the ground so that he wouldn't be running away. After withdrawing our blades from his fresh wounds, we simultaneously swiped them at his throat, and his head hit the floor, no longer attached.

Then the dust settled. It was very impressive.

"That was very impressive," I couldn't help but say aloud. "Good show."

"Best time I've had dispatching these guys for a while now." My mysterious ally sheathed their sword, and I my own. "Where are you headed next?"

"Location by the name of Fort Chaser," I replied. "Deeper behind enemy lines."

"You planning on looting this one at all?"

"Probably should, aye. Let's see what we can find."

The two of us took separate routes around this newly forcibly-deserted stronghold, taking note of the more valuable things that could be liquidated, and the more useful things that should stay behind for our own purposes.

"I say we could use this as a base," I suggested. "The emplacements are good, there's room for improvement, and plenty of things we can sell, too."

Selyn nodded. That was their name by the way, Selyn. Or so they told me. "Found a forge in the basement."

"That settles it, then," I concluded. "Granted, we will need to rebrand the place. The symbology present here isn't a great look."

"We'll keep at least one instance of each symbol and find display cases for them, like a museum or archive," Selyn recommended. "That way, there's record of what they turned these symbols into, so that others can know what to watch out for."

"Aye." Then I feel silent. Selyn could tell I was confused.

"Don't get to fight alongside others very often, do you?" Selyn asked.

"Never have before."

"Well, I'm always eager to make history."

"I'm not one to argue with witnessing it."

Avenger, Thyself Avenge

The words certainly one without even a sliver of the conviction that I possess would be ones to say that I should stay my hand when evil confronts me. It is creatures of evil, thieves of the earth and sky, sunderer of the land and sea, who would make me ashamed if they were my kin who demands tolerance of the intolerant. Though you have already heard me bestow great and terrible titles upon such walking enablers of suffering, I find myself willing only to make them known here upon this record, as someone like of such evil nature is beyond my good insults. Or at least, beyond hearing me call them by said curses.

It is people like my quarry who promote endlessly ideals of mercy towards the evil they perpetuate; you know the sort: Those who somehow manage to convince the hero who should be their bane, to spare them even after slaughtering endless thralls and pawns, and for some ungodly reason, *it works.* I can only wonder what insipid manipulation this oligarch will spew at me when I reach him, just as I wonder how shocked his final expression will be when it doesn't.

If you were to ask me what my greatest challenge on this road to the head of the snake I have paved with the bones of his thralls, it would be the insufferable others who seem to think it a grand idea to get in my way as soon as I pick up my sword. A lot of very pretentious people have come very close to death by being the sort to peddle the ignorance-promoting narratives that people like my target benefit from.

Be sure to dig two graves? Do you really think I'm planning to stop at just two evildoers?

Prove I'm better than him? I will, by personally throwing him into the jaws of the Nidhogg, along with everyone blind and stupid enough to follow him. They of course, have the option to run away once I get to them. They have the option to abandon his side and live the rest of their days in exile, deservedly unforgiven for siding with evil.

Granted, there is nothing wrong with using the tools of your enemies to benefit yourself, I understand that. But it's a risky play, one that risks your dignity and morality without strict moral and mental self-awareness and discipline. There's a difference between saying: "I didn't sign on for this." and "I was bad, but now I'm good." Only one of those is capable of being said without being a liar. And in case it isn't obvious, it's the former of those two.

How then to determine which is which, one might wonder? I cannot grant a universal answer to this question, only case-by-case instances. The lines can only be defined on that individual level, and there is no grand single answer that says when it is always the case that your once-clever plan to leech from your foe sees you turning into the very thing you would have otherwise sworn to destroy. But it is possible to do it right. How, one might ask? Again, case-by-case. I do not say this to avoid being the one to pass judgment on the matter. After all, I could easily find myself choosing who should live and die on that individual front, if you were to bring me the entire staff of a warehouse or supply depot flying the banner of the enemy.

But that is not the matter I deal with today. I deal with a more heinous creature than any who lives on the street: One who lives in the skyscraper. Of course, he wasn't in the skyscraper this time. I honestly do get tired of fighting on the same battlefields over and over again, more for how boring the tactics become than any weariness of battle with them and their thralls.

Of course, the main problem is that there are helipads on those skyscrapers they can use to flee, and I am only one man; I can't both advance up the stairways *and* fend off their evacuations simultaneously. Even though their mansions tend to have the things as well, they're more easily sabotaged than a high-rising one. So at least there's that.

Standing atop a hill that overlooked the cursed manse, my plan was in motion. What was I going to do? Just stand there, menacingly.

See, the funny thing about these areas is that even when you're not on privately owned land, they're still so scared of outsiders that they'll actually tell you you're not allowed to be there, even when by their own laws, that just doesn't fly. So I just stood there, and sure enough, someone from the manor came up to me to tell me I had to leave. But the thing is: I didn't. The quarry of mine in that stain upon the land passing as a house was just that scared of one man standing on a hilltop, looking down on him. I remained silent, just staring at the mansion with dismissiveness. Not even malice, just a very visible disdain that had sent the wastes of oxygen within into a state of pure panic. The guard who had come to me decided he had waited long enough, and then made the mistake of grabbing my hand with intent to cuff it. It earned him a fist to the throat, then the face, and then a kick to his knee to finish the job. The first strike sealed his fate, having crushed his windpipe and rendered breathing impossible. Death was assured. I dragged his crumpled, terminal form into a nearby bush and resumed my stance. The guy I just dealt with stopped coughing after a little under a minute.

The scent of fear within the manor was thick enough to cut with a knife. They knew they couldn't just end me from a distance; I wasn't trespassing yet. They also knew that, technically, all their man did was walk up to some guy and attack him; they could wipe their hands clean of the incident itself.

Then, something very interesting happened. A second person came up to me from the manor, inviting me to visit instead of telling me to leave. This had never happened before. At first, I figured he was simply trying to get me into the car so that he could do away with me quietly. I raised an eyebrow at him, giving a glare that without words told him that if he was lying to me, I would utterly destroy him. He seemed to be fully aware of that fact, and opened the passenger door of the car. That was an interesting sign. That he opened that door instead of the one behind it within the black van seemed to lend a kernel of truth to his claim that indeed this was an invitation.

As the van passed through the gate, my eyes darted all around, taking as many notes as possible. I may not get another chance to enter peacefully. That, or I may need to fight my way out. Unfortunately, my ability to retain numerical information is lackluster at best, so I just tried to remember *where* everybody was instead of how many there were. If I couldn't figure, I just used logic to determine where I might put one man or another in regards to this place's defense. From the looks of things, the front gate was the main defensive line. After that, a wide courtyard and lawn that would be quite difficult to cross in battle, given the openness of the terrain. Perhaps trench warfare might be necessary when besieging a location such as this. Unfortunately, I am only one man, and one man is not a trench-warfaring army. One man is an infiltrator to start lopping heads from within, or at least, I am. More and more, I began to figure that may be the best option.

Passing through the front door, I remembered my Diogenes: That in a rich man's house, there is nowhere to spit but his face. Granted, Diogenes would likely hate my guts for being such an edgelord at times, though 'at times' likely is too generous of a way to put it. At the very least, it gets things done, and beats the alternative for it.

I always do find myself filled with a primordial berserker rage every time I see one of those accursed novelty indoor signs; you know the ones, with some vomit-inducing generic milquetoast line that I dare not speak even in my own headspace, for its very utterance seems to sour the air around it. But you see those damned signs tainting the wallspace of a living room, common room or den with its insipid drivel and it just makes you want to tear the heads off the owners of the house.

Anyways... when I saw the metal 'live laugh love' sign

adorning the wall of the office that the mansion's absurdly rich owner was receiving me in, that's when I made my move.

As soon as the door closed, I whipped around and jabbed the guard who accompanied me in the throat, before grabbing the gun out of its holster and heaving it at the oligarch. He cursed as the metal frame smacked him in the head, distracting him from being able to grab the piece from his desk. After a *coup-de-grace* stomp to the guard's head, I grounded my quarry by slamming his face against a bookshelf, pretty much ensuring he remained in too much pain to take action against me.

I can only imagine the looks on the faces of the rest of the manor's security when they eventually re-entered the office to check on him and I was long gone already, having severed the head of the snake quite literally, and staking it to the tail of the last 'e' within that soulless phrase that only people without taste or imagination ever allow into their homes.

And then, it started to rain.

For this ultimate transgression of weather, this most contemptuous and undoubtedly worst-behaved type of climate, I found myself with no choice but to slaughter every single rain-based deity in every pantheon I could find.

I set about constructing shrines to each one to lure their earthly forms and make my declarations of war, my challenges to combat.

Tlaloc was first. Admittedly an ambitious choice, but if I wanted to send a message to the rest, this was where to start.

The process was not easy or quick, but soon I managed to gain an audience with Tlaloc, the Nahua supreme god of rain himself. I took him by surprise with my sudden and sure strikes. He had not the time to defend himself and soon fell to my blade. The rain immediately stopped where I stood. I had liberated myself. On to the next.

They would all soon learn this message in blood: I was the bane of the water that dares fall from the sky to ruin all plans and clothes alike.

The next to fall was Anzar, and fall he did, like Tlaloc, in the same manner, to the same trap that would claim Tó Neinilii and Ǫya before the rest of the pantheons began to catch on to my plans.

With four rain gods now dead by my hand, the rest could see the pattern pretty easily. I wondered if they would hide or run, or face me and fight. I truly had no prediction and my only plans were to continue my campaign of vengeance against the rain.

The next one to come to me did so riding the trail of a lightning bolt (as is the case for many rain deities) that struck the ground not far from where I stood. However, I recognized him. It was Tlaloc, the first one I'd killed. At least, he looked very similar.

"I thought I got you already?" I challenged him. "Do you mean to tell me that the rest are similarly not dead as well?"

Tlaloc said nothing. After placing his lightning channeling axe away, he only nodded.

"So I suppose the stopping of the rain whenever it happened was part of the act?"

Tlaloc nodded again to my question. I chuckled tiredly.

"What are you waiting for, then?" I challenged once more. "If not to fight me once again then to execute me for my crimes? It's quite clear the most I can do is annoy you to death...."

Tlaloc said nothing, his hand wrapped around the haft of the axe, as though he were about to draw it once more.

"Or perhaps you are *not* the one I've killed already but instead a similar deity with the same dominion?"

Tlaloc shook his head this time. At the very least, this meant he was indeed understanding and answering my questions. I rolled my shoulders and sighed before looking up at the sky. Though dark and cloudy, no rain fell.

"At least it's not raining as we have this little chat," I joked. Tlaloc nodded with a slight levity that quietly showed the humor of the comment was not lost on him.

"Are you going to execute me for my affronts and challenges, having assaulted and killed the bodies of four deities?" I asked. "It would make sense.... I did, after all, stray from the path I was walking."

To this, Tlaloc tilted his head in confusion.

"Everything I did *before* this vendetta against the rain, was... well, let's be honest. It was *right* to kill that decadent bastard in the mansion; it was *right* to impale his head on his own stupid and drab wall décor. But as soon as I was done with that, I rode that high straight off the path that I once swore to remain on."

Finally, Tlaloc had an opinion. It only took this long and this much bloodshed before the gods finally had something to say: "Have you?"

"True as it may be that I haven't *actually* killed any of you, the principles of my actions remain," I replied solemnly. "I strayed all the same and it would make sense to end me here and now for it, before that straying actually causes earthly consequences for my fellow man."

"Well," Tlaloc said. "Good thing you didn't actually kill any of us, then."

"I am curious, however," I admitted. "How close did I get? Did I cause a bruise, leave a mark, or barely even perturb?"

Tlaloc laughed hard at this curiosity of mine. "You... impressed."

A bolt of lightning struck the ground again, and Tlaloc vanished in its wake. Because I am no fool, I made sure to examine the crater the lightning left behind, to see if Tlaloc had left a memento of his visit, an artifact to mark the occasion.

Now then, a fool I may have been to fight the rain itself, but I'm more than willing to accept that I impressed its keepers with the fight I gave it. As much as I know my enemy is not the rain—or even necessarily the forces that ensure its fall—I cannot ignore how much it is my least favorite weather of them all. One might wonder if it was less that it was *rain*, and more that I had no means to effectively negate its detriments. If you asked me personally, I would say that because I had no such means, that was what ensured my disdain of it. And despite how much I hate the rain, I still could not help but be in awe at what one of its keepers had left behind:

His axe.

Those oligarchs are *fucked* now.

THE PLANET OF TIME

It is sweat, and not water, that one must ration and conserve above all else when they must survive in the Desert, where prosperity is as fiction as opportunity. Dunes that act as doldrums of the land and of existence itself, that must be traversed in the night, when the air is not so blazing and hostile as the sun. Canyons are sought in the night, to take shelter within during the day. And so the cool solitude of the night proves itself ally, and sun proves the enemy. Through canyon into cavern, for the underground within the earth is the place of ultimate shelter from the world above and its ravages.

But beyond desert must lie mountains, for rock must become somewhere... and so the ascent may cut the air in half and then quarters, but it is the essence of Training to hone oneself in the Heights, and the fire in the blood thusly burns brighter, its intensity the essence of Precision; when Precision can be achieved, even though the air is thin and hostile.

Though tiring is the pursuit of Precision in such a perpetually hostile air that takes more energy than it is possible for it to give, an eternal deficit whose payoff is as existent as opportunity.

The Stone sags into the earth, as tired of remaining

constantly as the ground beneath it is tired of supporting more weight than should ever be asked of it, though seemingly it remains without the decency to just fall already.

Unknown is why the walls remain so unnaturally existent, whether spite or contempt, it remains a mystery. Unknown is which side of the walls is better to stand within, for the information of what lies on the other side is so heavily obscured by the stone that refuses to crack.

But the Stone is irrelevant, and as are the walls. They are paid no mind, as should be. The escape from the Desert is all that matters. The Desert indeed, where fortune is a mirage, a mocking image that dances before the eyes with no purpose other than the grandiose taunt that it is.

What then, when the only solace that survival seems to grant is simply adding more seconds to the time that was spent within? Moreover, will escape from the Desert even grant solace, or will the denizens of what greener fields lie beyond despise the one who clawed his way out of purgatory itself, for they were not already part of the clique?

It matters not, for the Desert was left behind, and that will be all that matters in the end for he who must escape The Planet of Time.

The Planet of Time: Where each day feels as nine or ten, or more. Every second wasted upon The Planet of Time ticks minutes off the clock of life's span, and time runs faster towards being out completely.

The Planet of Time: Where death has not the decency to be swift, but instead demands of itself the slowest and most drawn-out of dismal fate for all those trapped within, who want nothing but out.

And so The Planet of Time consumes Time itself,

engulfing its prized prey with claws digging inches deep into the flesh of the tired and weary, whose talons no longer burn, for nerves are deadened by sheer grey dullness that has consumed all else.

Why then does it bother on? When the damned and denied no longer can amuse with their pained reactions, why then does The Planet of Time bother to continue? What point is there in it?

The Planet of Time must die. For all these reasons, for all this incomprehensible contempt and all this unfounded stomping and screeching, it must die.

The Planet of Time must die, along with those who made it such.

The Planet of Time must die for having so drained every part of its own self, where even to begin with its list of crimes who number more than the atoms that give it form?

How even to attempt comprehension, when the mind is so thoroughly spent that it cannot seem to force itself to continue, the fumes and sputters of what once was a working engine groaning under the weight of its imminent collapse, and the knowledge that it must not?

That it must not fall... that I must not fall. The Planet of Time cannot be what I allow to kill me.

But how can blood be drawn from a stone?

How can time be reclaimed from the singularity that does nothing but swallow it?

How can purpose be found in a world so empty?

Purpose, it seems, has become as fiction of an idea as chances to discern it, let alone fulfill it. Such is the planet, and thus why it must die. Without thought, it damns all else to thoughtlessness and agony as unprecedented as it is appalling that nothing is done against it.

Those who would stand against it are condemned to watch all others do nothing, and watch as the chances to prove their valor pass by and old age takes them, with no stories to their name and no deeds to prove that they were of honor.

On the Planet of Time, honor is similarly fiction as are chances to prove its value, as are chances of any regard. Opportunity itself has become a hoax here, and reason shares this occupancy in nonexistence.

The Desert here is marked not by the sandy dunes or blazing winds, but the sheer absence of life that the planet creates. Though the process of living existence may be undergone, existence is only just existence, and life has become as fiction as the chance to live it.

The Planet of Time may not be of only sandy dunes of stagnation and scorching winds slamming as hard as brick walls against progress, but it may as well be, for the brick walls have not even the decency to stand still, that one day they may be climbed over or broken through, but instead it chooses to charge against reason as it adds to its height to make it more impossible to scale, and adds more to its width to make it more impossible to demolish, sprinting to create as cramped a cage as possible at speeds that should not be capable of existing, and the only passion of the planet is zealous contempt, in its screeching and screaming stampede against anything other than itself and its favor, the screeching and grinding wail speeding along the sands of the Desert, its speed unmatched in hunting and crushing the very notion of endeavor.

The Planet of Time must die. Time must not be wasted

debating how much more complicated the matter is than it may seem, for so long as the fight within the ranks rages, the one assurance is that the enemy is not being stopped.

The Planet of Time is not being stopped when those who would stand against it are held back by the willfully ignorant who demand negligence in the name of useless scrutiny.

Though scrutiny and skepticism are themselves inherently far from a waste of time, there are times indeed when it becomes no more than a dragged weight, a chain that binds arms out of reach of action. Sometimes, it is to benefit. Other times, to stagnate and downright assure that the crimes of the planet continue.

The Planet of Time must die. There can be no doubt. There can be no delay, and there can be no time wasted waiting on permission from the very purveyors of evil who would be the ones to ensure that the planet lives forever in its wretched path, forever crushing all things into the Grey Dust of Order.

Faith cannot be placed in the planet, nor the breathless demons who purport to apotheosis, the invisible justifiers of endless horror masquerading as gods. It is in the virtues of logic, reason, and honor that those who will assure the just doom of the planet will place their minds. Not blind faith to breathless non-entities that frustratingly demand reverence and perception of perfection, and even more frustratingly, their followers accept such insane claims to absolute omniscience as the cowards and death-deservers they are. To kill The Planet of Time, the heads of these snakes must be cut from their necks, and not even the crows should feast upon their carcasses, for sustaining such noble creatures is far too good for them. The faith-mongering hordes are lower than the dung beetle, and only gnats and flies should be what scavenge their husks, unceremoniously dumped into the Desert they sentenced all others who weren't part of their clique to. They must die without ceremony, and they must be given not even a headstone or marker for their graves to become shrines to their mindless devotees. Ideally, the devotees have met the same fate.

The Planet of Time must die, as must its purveyors and benefactors. If it does not, there are no words in any mortal or immortal language alike that can describe the sheer fall that awaits. There are no opulent adjectives; none can be brought to bear. There are no grand adverbs; the planet does not deserve to have prose wasted on describing the threat to existence itself that its continued existence poses. Nothing can describe what will be, should The Planet of Time be allowed to continue its cursed existence, because nothing will be. Nothingness is the very essence of the planet, and not even in the profound manner of the Book of the Void, where in the absence of interference, instinct sharpened becomes perfected action. On The Planet of Time, sparks are forbidden. On The Planet of Time, sparks are stomped out with screeching fervor, and The Planet of Time itself lets out the tantrum yell of the most comical infant as it does so.

The skills that dictate what one must do in the Desert, the know-how and cleverness that tells how sweat and not water is what must be conserved, they matter not in the face of the sheer unending nature of the planet. On The Planet of Time, the only reward for adversity is more adversity. The only reward for pulling through is more that must be pulled through. The only thing cleverness means to the planet, is that the meat can be ground for longer. The only reward on the planet is more of it. For this, The Planet of Time must die, more urgently than ever. The only payment for the share that is given is demand of more. The Planet of Time knows nothing else but to cause all skill, all effort and all drive to be wasted away, wasted on its life force, wasted on becoming the fuel that allows it further existence.

And so though The Planet of Time must die, I find myself no longer willing to put forth my share to its end, because I have put forth more than I should have for a dozen lifetimes. If after all this, there is still so much nothing, I refuse to bother further, and so I will no longer waste my time doing what should have been done already by cowards of inaction and head-bowing wastes of breath that infest the planet and permit its continuance. My contribution can only be to its starvation through my refusal to sacrifice anything more of my own to the Desert, my unwillingness to grant it anything other than famishment.

Today, I feel like I am the last man of honor. Tomorrow, I will feel like I am the just euthanasia of all. And beyond that... I will feel nothing, and I will be glad to feel nothing, because at the very least, The Planet of Time died.

This is how all the dark prophecies start, isn't it? It seems I have prepared for a doom that will never come, but this is not to my fortune. Am I cursed to never be given the chance to fight it? Am I doomed to see all chances of valor escape me? To die of Time's decay, before such a chance is even born? With no glory to call my own, no stories....

I cannot tell which would be crueler: That fate meeting me in my youth or my dusk?

All I know is that I cannot, I must not, be inflicted this

fate. I must not. The shame would be immeasurable... but how? How do I defy this fate, without also becoming the very corruption I would have otherwise sworn to destroy? How would I balance the refusal to willful ignorance, the capital dishonor, with the demands of reason, sanity, and justice without charging headlong into corruption's awaiting grasp?

How do I kill The Planet of Time, without damning my name to be among the countless who simply killed *for* it instead? I can feel the grand and constant calls for me to fall, to break and crumble.... The Planet of Time eagerly awaiting my surrender, my fall to it and its horrid wishes. It awaits the news that I can no longer fight it, that I would join it and its benefactors in its evil....

I can feel the longing for my corruption, the chance to make me a champion of darkness; and not the good kind of darkness, the shadows you walk alongside and wield to your ends. I understand that the shadows can be ally just as much as the sun can be enemy. I know this well but the darkness the planet beckons me to align with...? Those shadows are not the Shadowed Path I walk.

How quickly would I be touted their exemplar, hoisted high upon a pedestal for fascists to worship, and good men to repulse from?

The Planet of Time must die, there can be no doubt. It must, so that no longer will I be so plagued by these visions of my doom, that even if I live through, I would not survive, because in my surrender, my honor would die a most painful death indeed.

The Planet of Time must die instead, for there is no sweat left to ration for its Desert, and I refuse to allot it any more. I will throw no more darts over a wall to a target on the other side with the scorekeeper asleep. I will expend nothing further.

But this is how the dark prophecies always start, isn't it? With these declarations, do I doom myself to endless scrutiny by manipulators and traitors who disguise themselves as allies?

If nothing else, when the messages come flooding in, when the cavalcade of insipid quotes, vomit-inducing dross-resemblant so-called motivation, and prying questions begin, at least I will know who my allies really are. Or rather, who they are not.

Merciful Morons
Need Not Apply

The holy city of the wretched, that men of reason repulse at and gladly take up arms to make rubble. Better known as our next target.

Word had already spread like wildfire across the world about how we had only months before, destroyed a different sanctum for fascism, single-handedly ending the lives of its entire ruling class within a day and letting the people do the rest. I would say we cut the head off the snake but that would be an insult to snakes.

Our route passed by a familiar hill with a collapsed mine entrance in its side. Nobody yet had broken through the wall of stone we left behind to guard the world-killer that lay within. Perhaps it would not kill the world but the possibility was far too likely to be ignored. Perhaps another day, in a far-future age, such an artifact will be ready to meet a world that would use it for more altruistic purposes than humans are capable of mustering.

"Should we?" Sykar asked.

"Good question," Argus responded. "If there were a city that needed such leveling, it would be the one we head to now."

"If we do choose to wield it against them, we must all agree to reseal it within the mine and never even look upon the hill for at least a hundred years," the Night Witch proposed.

All eyes soon turned to me, who had yet to voice his opinion. I had been mulling it over since the Hidden Hill came back into our sight. I had been wondering if we should make this one bastion of our enemies the exception.

"Do we trust ourselves to hold to that oath?" I asked the group but mainly the Night Witch, as it was her who had made the proposition itself. "If we do use it against Aurophile City, will we be able to bring ourselves to return it to its resting place?"

"Or will we succumb to the temptation to use it against the rest of our enemies?" Sykar finished my thought and I nodded in response. Not as in a 'yes we will succumb' response but that he had, in fact, said what I was thinking and had yet to word.

We all paused and stared at the stones which covered the entrance to the mine.

"It would not be too difficult to clear the entrance," Argus noted. "Perhaps we should at least take the artifact so that someone else does not stumble upon it later. A collapsed mine entrance begs the curious and the adventurous to clear it of rubble and inevitably discover what lies within."

I then realized something. "These are not the same rocks that we buried this place with," I informed everyone and we immediately began clearing the stones. It had become clear that someone else had been here and sealed the mine just as we did. But did they do it to hide the artifact or cover their tracks after taking it? That much we needed to know. Whether or not to wield it against our enemies would have to wait, assuming it still remained hidden here. By the time we gained access to the chamber that held what myself, Argus, and Sykar nearly had a shootout over, our relief was palpable that the artifact was still there.

"Did none of you pay attention to the foot tracks here?" the Night Witch asked. "Whoever was here last went down the wrong path and gave up halfway before resealing the place."

"Have we led someone to this spot?" I asked, turning towards the way we'd come.

"We haven't been followed at all," Sykar mentioned. "Perhaps this mysterious seeker gave up for good."

"Why reseal the entrance, then? With what is down here, you'd think they'd just come back another day with more supplies and better preparedness," Argus wondered aloud.

"Perhaps whoever was here last knew what was down here and resealed the entrance specifically to ward off other seekers of the artifact and also to obscure their intrusion from us," I postulated.

"At the very least, I think the decision has been made for us," the Night Witch concluded. "This place's secret is no longer between the three of you. At *least* two others know of this place and what is here, myself included."

"Agreed," I said, grabbing the artifact that had once almost spelled mutual destruction for us and pocketing it. "Whether or not we wield it against Aurophile City remains to be decided but I do know this much: It cannot remain here."

Everyone else nodded solemnly, rightfully keeping a

watchful eye on me. I nodded back to tell them that it was a good thing they were doing so.

We all agreed to head towards the city of our foes that we had been planning to make our next mark anyway; we would make the decision once we arrived: Whether or not to turn the city to dust with the power that rested in my pocket. Dust or rubble, we also understood that whatever we chose regarding the artifact's use, it could not remain out and about within the world. Even if we could be trusted to choose when and where to wield its great and terrible power, its very existence would invite the very people we swore to destroy to wrest it from our hands by any means necessary—the more dishonorable the methods, the more likely to be employed.

Therein lies the one thing that has confused me so much about the humans almost more than anything else, if not the most baffling fact about them entirely: The human allergy to decency. The sheer love of evil they have and how vehemently they repulse at the idea of honor. How could such a species be permitted to continue so vile an existence in a universe that supposedly is good? To do so goes against the very nature of what would claim to be of the light... if the light even was what it claimed to be.

And there another, how the humans defile all they touched. Light and dark alike matter not to the eyes of a human, who only wants to know which one will more easily erase those different from themselves from existence, for as surely as the sun and moon will rise and set, humans are evil in nature, and wish only destruction and death upon that which is different.

So perhaps the artifact should be used to finally rid the world and the stars of their weight? Or is it more the case, that simply by the nature of my acknowledging this fact, I must never be permitted to even lay eyes on such a decisive power? How utterly and completely human evil truly has ruined all if I can no longer be sure of any of my actions, just because the humans keep ruining the name of action itself. Does this lend further argument that their existence must end or does it only further justify that *mine* must instead?

We are surrounded at all times by only enemies but does that make the one who stands alone the one truly wrong? Or am I the last bastion of reason among lovers of administering empty death?

I wondered if this was a side effect of the artifact, this debate that raged on in my mind as I, Sykar, Argus, and the Night Witch traveled across the desert plains for three days making our way towards Aurophile City.

If I am the last bastion of honor, then I do what honor demands. And honor demanded that I make no secret of the toll bearing this artifact was taking of me.

I took the item out of my pocket and studied it at our campfire, inviting my compatriots to do the same.

"Know thy enemy, they always say," I said. "Well, here's one."

"That item is the essence of why madness reigns," Sykar conjectured. "I wonder if something like that is resting at the heart of Aurophile City and keeping it the horrid way it is."

"If true, then that item is what will liberate the world from its presence," Argus added. "Perhaps upon flattening that citadel of capitalistic greed, we should destroy what destroyed it."

I nodded in agreement. "If we do use it to that end,

we should destroy it afterwards. If nothing else, it will silence the conflict it creates... and I find it hard to believe that would be a bad thing."

"To do so also silences the temptation to continue using it to turn our enemies to dust," the Night Witch furthered the point. "But if we don't use it, if we take down Aurophile City the old fashioned way, do we continue to keep it just in case we find something worse?"

"I can't imagine much things worse than that damned city." Argus scoffed. "If there's anything that artifact should be used on, we're less than a day's travel from it now. If we hold onto our royal flush for too long, we risk the game ending before we can play it."

We all pondered the fire and the device in my hand.

"We all know that we wouldn't be wrong to use that thing on Aurophile City," Argus continued. "The thing that's got us tied up right now is us wondering if we need to save it for something worse. Hell, if something worse rises out of the ashes of Aurophile City like an evil phoenix, we can slap that thing again and turn *it* to dust next. If not, we put a boot or bullet into it to make sure it can't harm anyone else, for better *and* for worse."

I nodded, silently agreeing with Argus, just as silently hoping that I would have the strength to do what needed to be done. And I didn't mean the strength to level Aurophile City with this thing; no, that was trivial. I hoped I had the strength to put my boot or a bullet into it once the bastion of evil was no more. We all knew that though this artifact's use was effectively unlimited, we would need to limit ourselves in its use, lest we would build the next city that those like us would want nothing more than to tear down. We could not allow ourselves to become this, honor demanded it.

I looked at the city of our ire over the ridge, only a few hours walk away. The sun was due to rise soon but my patience was no more. My companions seemed to see this in my eyes and they all stood up with me.

I was about to open my mouth and tell them they needed not follow me but I knew well that they should, just in case I could not do what needed to be done. If I failed to meet the demands of reason, between four of us, someone would surely be able to.

We all walked in silence towards the opulent gates of Aurophile City and I wonder if I could be proud of the fact that despite the power in my hands, the power that would let me seize this temple of capital instead of destroy it, I still found myself disgusted by the very existence of those walls and that accursed gate, and still found it a blight upon the land. The warnings from the watchtowers rang out in the night, that we were to leave or be shot, because we weren't part of the clique. As if I needed any further reminders as to why this place and everyone in it needed to be pulverized.

I looked to Sykar. He nodded. I looked to Argus. He nodded. I looked to the Night Witch. She nodded. I raised the artifact in my hand, and suddenly the red dots on our chests shut off as shouts from the guards ordered that the gate be opened to us. This was most confusing.

The gates of Aurophile City swung open, offering all of the troves within as our prize for having brought so grand a power to its door. We were being invited into the clique, offered all the benefits of the club, and now we had a problem. As I looked upon my compatriots again, we all shared in this shock and confusion. This was a twist of fate indeed, one we had not anticipated. We had planned for all kinds of enemies to beset us, we had planned for every manner of hostility. We had planned to be proven right in every way that this city must die. And until this moment, all this planning was to our benefit. We were so startled by the sudden pacification of our enemies, that we didn't know what to do. Were they surrendering? Were they trying to trick us? Had they, against all odds, made a legitimate offer?

"How do we know if it's a trick?" I asked my allies.

They were silent.

"Guys... how do we know if it's a trick?"

Nobody had an answer. All eyes were on me, and the pulsing power of the retribution for all the sundered lands and lives that I stood prepared to command to make true the doom of all our foes. One decision separated us from fate.

"Is it a trick?" I finally pleaded to the three companions at my side.

"The city's called Aurophile," Argus reminded.

"The doors opened when we proved we held something valuable," the Night Witch also reminded.

"They know who we are and what we've done," Sykar furthered. "The only reason it'd be legitimate is as a bribe."

"It's your call, Talon," the Night Witch said to me. "Like it or not, the choice is yours. How do *you* know if it's a trick?"

Time seemed to slow to a crawl and eventual halt as my mind raced at untold speeds; with the kind of power in my hand, time very likely *was* slowing down, just to give me the chance to more carefully consider my next words, and what actions would follow. As my eyes darted around, taking in every detail they could, I felt like I was moving faster than anything else in the universe. I looked to the three warriors I had depopulated fascist citadels alongside before. I looked into the city before us, and I felt disgust at its opulence. Once again, I almost felt comforted by the fact I still recoiled at this beacon of greed in the middle of a dying world, whose skyscrapers, monuments to capitalism, would slow the very planet's orbit like drag fins sprouting from the very ground, deliberate in their design to add a few microseconds to the days, just to make the workers work for a microsecond or two more, for no reason other than contempt. Practicality was lost to a place like this.

I could see the futures unravel in my mind, futures that only awaited my decision for which path to walk. I could declare to my companions that our fight was over, we had won, and this city was our prize. I could turn on them, using the artifact to instead make myself the only one who would claim that prize. Or I could do what was right, and show this city the same mercy it would have granted us, the same mercy that we had shown to countless of our foes, and the foes of the world: None at all.

With one raising of my hand, and one will coursed through the Stone of Fate, the great wave of energy finally released itself, and my will became known: *Only my enemies die today.*

And so the golden city was torn asunder. Words could not describe the sheer elation of seeing all those wealthy, corrupt denizens die; there was no greater honor than to bring forth their doom. My only regret is that I could not make their ends more painful.

I Will Walk

the Shadowed Path

f there is anything that can know the name of every god in the astral sea and every demon in the burning hells, the mushrooms would be the ones to possess that knowledge. The hardiest beings I have ever encountered, to call them extremophiles would be a sore understatement, for when nothing else shall grow, the mushrooms shall. We live in the shadow of the harbingers of the end of decay, for their presence is what marks the end of nightmares. When the mushrooms do not grow, only doom awaits where even they shall not sprout.

And so imagine my surprise when upon this patch of void-tainted ground, where it seemed the very universe bore a gaping and bleeding wound, the mycelium colony was still there, defiant of the will of the Realm of the Unrealm, where all that crosses its threshold becomes the nothingness within, but even with this sheer gap in the very fabric of existence, the mushrooms grew.

Those who curiosity claims shelter in the minds of, find themselves wondering what power the Void Spores possess; would such power be inherited upon those who would consume it?

The hands of the Void, The Space Between Them, reach long and far into the realms of mortal reality and unreality alike. To wield this power is to know it like no other with the sheer reach of its domain, and the sheer feats that its harnessing permits and guarantees. And for those with the skill to wield it, and the discipline to control it, it can become what legends are made of, what history is written of, what statues are built for, and what monuments are dedicated to.

For those without... the Void claims them without thought or consequence. That which was them becomes part of the nothingness, and their existence is only of the Void's.

How then, to ensure that if the Void is the power we shall wield, shall we do so in the manner of the legends, statues and monuments, whilst not becoming one with the Void and being consumed by its emptiness?

There is a difference between emptiness and nothingness, and the Void is emptiness. In Nothingness, there is a power of its own but the Void is what beckons to me today, and thus I must ask my questions of the Void.

The Void's answers, once again, left much to be desired, for the Void did not answer. It merely continued to exist in its natural state of unnatural existence. It is most inconvenient, as answers tend to be helpful, in my experience.

And so I am left with its messengers, the part of our universe that spanned from one into the other, the impossible fungi that grew upon the patch of Void, and though cautious as I was about such phenomena, I had to wonder if the incredible were possible. It was a wonder that had been all but squandered in the age of Grey. That I found myself wondering once more at last, it certainly did tell me that perhaps the Void was onto something.

In the Void lay the power to drive the Grey back into the unfathomable abyss from whence it came. I know I would rather be in hell than purgatory, because hell is a realm beyond consequence. You can fight hell, but purgatory's greatest trick is the overwhelming consequence that arises from all actions within, that drive all lines to their dullest, most boring outcome possible. There is a difference between uninteresting, and *boring.* The boredom won't kill you, but it will make you wish it could, and it truly does feel as though a drill is boring through your mind, lobotomizing as much as it can and shredding into pulp what makes oneself themselves by halting all progress and event, blending the entire mass into an unrecognizable sludge, until all that remains in one's own skull is a pile of decrepit slurry that used to be a mind.... That is indeed exactly what the Burning Grey feels like.

In the wake of the grinding grey and burning stagnation, I feel as though my arms have become but toothpicks in width, with strength just as paltry, that no amount or intensity of training can rectify. In the wake of the slow fall to oblivion, I have found myself wondering: Is it that my strength has left me, or did I even possess any to begin with? In the absolute absence of any chance or opportunity to test or prove myself, the doubt that there was anything there in the first place is inevitable. I cannot tell if there is any part of me of note, whether in body, mind, or morals. Whether I am as plain and uninspired as the grey skies above the cities of this wretched century of stagnation is a question, it seems, I can never answer. And so... I must assume the negative. I cannot delude myself into thinking I am more than what I am, even as I know nothing of what I am, the safe bet is to assume that I am nothing... and not even the kind that makes a man more powerful than any other; that, too, would be nice, wouldn't it? Rather than the nothing that means I have nothing to lose, it is the nothing that means there is nothing to be gained. Opportunity is as fictional as prosperity, a grand conspiracy and sheer joke that the entire world is in on, that for some reason is able to make its perpetrators still roar with laughter despite how dull, boring, uninspired and utterly mindless in nature the joke is. It is indeed just like them to mindlessly ramp up the madness of no purpose and no point.

Comprehension and mindfulness has been my only weapon against the sheer crushing weight of the time that time forgot, until I may find a new weapon to wield against my foes who are too cowardly to fight me in battle, and instead exile themselves to hiding and waiting. Long have I waited for what would allow me to take the fight to them. Long have I waited for the weapon that would finally put into my hands, my fate and the power to ruin the lives of the wicked whose continued lives only testify to the ignorance of the gods and a counterargument to the very idea of decency and honor.

In the Void, I have found that weapon. Delivered to me by way of the fungi that learned. They learned and in their steps I follow, bearing witness to the Void becoming a part of me as I did carefully imbibe their power, at no small risk to myself and my sanity, much less my life. But the power is part of me now, and I have answered the question of if I would take that risk with a resounding 'yes.'

I have taken the step into the unknown and have come out the other side as exactly what I needed to become. A pity that it took this long but better late than never.

Pity not that my burden now becomes to wield such a risky power, nor that there are better ways to make one's stand. Spare me your pity; I have no use for it. If you must drain your own energy on pity, then do so toward that which it took for me to make my life my own. Something so otherworldly and forbidden that it should come to this, instead of life just being in one's own hands from the start as it should be. Pity that it took this long, and because of that delay, I may be condemned to never be able to enact enough vengeance in a thousand lifetimes to bring me peace. Even then, I don't mind the quest. If this is what I am, then so be it. I could be much worse.

Long have I wondered if when the day of my chance came, would I even still be me? Not even whether or not I would still be myself at the end of it all, but would I still even be who I am when the beginning finally took place, if even it did? Would the infuriating machinations of a world so senselessly cruel and cruelly stagnant have ground my brain smoother than a river stone, so much so that no longer could I even register that the chance had come? Would my muscles even have the strength left to lift my arm to grasp it?

The Void's ambassadors have brought me the chance I longed for when I saw them upon the tear in reality, and I knew I would be a fool not to take it. That it would come to such desperation, that this shadowed path is what I take for even the chance of clawing my way into the light? It is as unsurprising as it is... I would say 'regrettable,' but that feels too weak a word. I can no longer conjure the brainpower to think of a stronger one. Such is what the grinding has done to me, and what the Void promises I will reclaim.

Stagnation has not the decency to pause or halt

progress, instead dragging it backwards in regression born of rust. The chains twist and crack, flakes of their form scattering as deadly powder in every direction, the cancerous plague of decay and necrosis that becomes what they touch.

They have not the decency to bind in ways that can be seen or struck.

If the Void is the only voice that promises the power to break them and their binders, then the Void is the call I will heed. Where then will my nemeses hide, when the shadows they believed their haven are where I await them? Nowhere will be hidden from me, for the Void is the power I shall wield.

I have grown weary of my constant lust for vengeance, and now the Void grants me this chance, this power to finally fulfill all of those sleepless dreams of seeing the wretched die in agony, and maybe, at long last, my hatred may finally rest.

I used to doubt I would ever find peace, no matter how much vengeance I brought. I used to dread that no number of severed heads of the wicked would satisfy. Now I know better, and I know that to do so would indeed allow me to find solace. My dread of late has been instead that I will never know peace because rather than never being satisfied in vengeance, I will never know the chance to enact it.

But the Void has promised me that chance, and so I will take it. Grouse at me if you must that I will not wield a more righteous power, but if that power wished my allegiance, it should have made itself known to me long ago.

I swore once, long ago, that I would know when to cross at a ford, though I did not have those exact words for it; I knew that I would be a fool to stay at harbor when the day of need came, even if all others and everything I had known stayed behind. Though I did not know that these were the words I know reaffirm, I swore that I would know the soundness of my ship and the favor of the day when it came. That when the sirens blared, when the fires were raging, and the need was now, I would not be unprepared. Another oath among the many that will ensure that at the end of this path, I will prove the victor; this Void, though it is my power and though its allure to madness and corruption is grand, will not be what ends me. It will not be what dictates my fall from either honor or life itself.

The mushrooms know the names of gods and demons alike, and my name is neither. I am not a warrior sent by hell or heaven, I am not born of angel or devil, and so I am not bound by their failings and their weaknesses. They know their names, revealing to me my targets, the giants I must bring to fall, whose weight must be liberated from the tired shoulders of the world, as their lungs shall be liberated of breath.

I can hear their voices, whispering to me from the Void, that chills my blackest heart, that steels my readied mind, that strengthens my hand and conditions my bones for battle, whether in the fields or in the streets, and with the broken ends of bottles that may be all that I have left.

The power of the Void is mine to wield. They shall fall.

From hatred, my will to avenge is born, tempered by discipline that shall ensure my honor, even as I wield this power that few can know without succumbing to madness. I am willing to believe myself among the few, for to do otherwise would guarantee my fall, because I already know that in the Void I must find my strength, for no other path or power presents itself to me. Mindfulness shall be my sword against ignorance; vigilance, my shield against madness. The symphonies of battle, verses like oaths coursing through my veins and turning blood into fire, whose smoke will cloud the vision of my foes until I render their weapons moot and rend the flesh from their bones and their heads from their necks.

My brutality will be known upon they who believe themselves invincible, and not even the crows shall feast upon their husks, for to sustain such noble creatures is a privilege my foes—the builders of the iniquitous towers—do not deserve; they are lower than the dung beetle, and they will meet the most painful fates that I will consider myself honored to administer. They shall learn what comes of a mind like my own with nothing better to do than dream up the most painful of deaths for the most deserving of foes, and has now finally found its chance—a chance, *any* chance—to make things right. With my readiness to dedicate my life to the cause of ending theirs, they will know the bone-chilling fear and uncertainty that came with my taking on of the Void's power and, that to their horror, I do not join their side in evil.... The difference between them and I is that I passed my trial to wield this power, and my knowledge that it is in power's wielding that decides its morality will act as but one of uncountable buffers that will ensure that in my eternity as the warrior-wanderer who took upon the Void to wield against his foes, that no matter how many battles I shall fight and how many foes I shall slay, I will always remain true to who I am and who I have always wanted to be.

I will walk the shadowed path to claw my way into the light.

RETRIBUTION DONE RIGHT
DEFIES THE CYCLE

Not everyone has the strength to set the world on fire, or even just a single city. But we had, and the elation was as grandly euphoric as it was harrowing.

The Artifact worked. Aurophile City, and all of its inhabitants, were dust in the wind, the four of us staring at the crater that was left with mixed emotions. Retribution for its existence had been delivered long overdue and we felt unbreakable for it. With that feeling of invincibility soon came the harrowing realization that we felt as though the pride of a thousand victories were coursing through our veins. Because with that feeling comes the itch to feel it again, and the Artifact that we just used to make it happen was the very manifest of that temptation. Or rather, the Artifact that I had just used, and was still in my hand.

Without a second to spare for thought, I slammed it on the ground and began stomping on it repeatedly, like I would the head of an oligarch. I desperately smashed it to pieces, kicking away the fragments and continuing to destroy the larger pieces, not sparing a second for any thought process other than the sheer need to destroy it.

The others looked to me as if I had entered the kind of trance one does in battle, when thought and action become as one, but instead of corrupt and morally destitute humans, my target was the very weapon that had just killed so many of them. I granted not a second's worth of breath-catching to allow doubt to even think of entering my mind as I did what I did, as I crushed the Artifact into the dirt, burying it like it had just buried a bastion of evil only moments before.

Eventually, the Artifact was in enough pieces that no one could ever hope to remake or reassemble it. Its time truly had passed, and no longer could even the most righteous souls that may ever walk this world wield its terrifying power.

"No time to wait," I told my companions as I caught my breath. "No time to let waiting beget doubt."

"We know," the Night Witch reassured. "We know."

We camped that night on the hill that overlooked what once was a city, now a crater.

"I cannot count the number of ways we would have been corrupted by that thing if you had not done what you did, Talon," Argus commented as we sat around the fire that night with food and drink. Travel rations they may have been, but unlike most, they didn't taste like hardtack and swill. "Every time I think of what we may have tried to do to keep our minds and morals safe despite its continued existence, it always arrives at some dark conclusion."

"Which outcome happens more, do you figure?" Sykar curiously asked, with a touch of levity to lighten things up a little in the face of all those dark timelines we had avoided. "Between us tearing each other to shreds for control of it, or us getting corrupted by its power and wielding it again and again and becoming the very enemies we destroyed today?"

"The former," Argus answered and the Night Witch nodded as Argus amended: "Well, more like a combination of the two."

"Probably one of us goes power-mad, the rest either get killed by them or kill them and repeat the cycle until there's only one left," the Night Witch surmised.

"Every time it ends with only one of us remaining, that one either becomes the kind of overlord we've spent our whole lives putting the heads of on pikes, or smashes the thing against the ground like we should've done. Or rather, like what Talon *did* do today," Argus continued.

I remained silent as I contemplated their words.

"I can see in my mind's eye how each of us could succumb, or how each of us would remain the last bastions of morality in the face of the corruption of the rest. All those paths that lead to only one survivor, and whichever path that last survivor takes, I feel as though I can see them all. And just as I can see them all, I can take solace in all of them simultaneously since Talon had the strength to so quickly ensure that *none* of those darker timelines are the one we will walk."

Argus' words were true, and I get the feeling we *all* could see those timelines, he was just the one to put them in words.

"I can at least see mine," the Night Witch began. "Whether corruption or conscience, I can see them both. Whether slitting everyone else's throats in the night to take possession, or watching us each succumb one after the other to what that thing could do…. And in the end, I won't lie, I can't see a timeline in which I did the right thing when I was the sole survivor."

It takes great strength to admit your lack of immunity to corruption, and to be able to acknowledge that on the day of decisions and in the time of need, you might not be able to do the right thing, when the thing that benefits you directly so much more than honor could ever do. We all could silently know these things, but the Night Witch showed rare strength in her willingness to claim it.

Not to be outdone, Sykar soon said his piece: "Hell, I can see how I'd fall... probably challenging Talon to a duel for control of the thing, then landing some dirty shot to finish him and take possession. Paranoia would soon take me, and I'd preemptively kill you two just to avoid someone doing to me what I did to him. After who knows how many more cities I'd level... maybe I'd throw it on the ground and introduce it to my boot as well, but something dark tells me that I'd only do it to stop someone else from having it, and destroy it in my final breaths out of spite."

Sykar sighed and rolled his shoulders. "Words cannot express how relieved I am that we will never see me lose my honor so completely, so utterly. Much as here and now I know that I'd be counting on someone to kill me if I was so far gone... if I was so far gone, that someone else in my brain pretending to be me would be using all my skill and cleverness to make me believe that I was still the same, and everyone *else* had lost their way."

Sykar's left arm shivered as he seemed to try to work out a minor cramp in his shoulder, but it was more likely the shivers of realization that he could have very easily walked that path had my actions not prevented it. "I owe you my life, Talon, though it may never seem like it in a hundred years of this timeline in which you did the right thing from the start.”

"The greatest victories are sometimes the ones no one will ever know," Argus offered. "Though Aurophile City's destruction is indeed the most *major* victory we have achieved, the *greatest* one is that we will never walk those darker paths, wielding the guise of protectionism that barely veils sheer amorality.”

"Interesting choice of words," the Night Witch commented, after taking a swig of her drink.

"Couldn't think of any better ones." Argus shrugged. "Talon? You've been silent this whole time, and yet it's you we have to thank for the fact that these dark futures will never be ours.”

I took a drink from my flask. "Everything you've all said is true and correct, and I am glad that we will not walk those paths of corruption. But I carry a strange and unique burden as the one who called upon that power, who leveled Aurophile, and who felt *elated* to watch all those oligarchs be vaporized.”

"Don't tell me you feel *ashamed* to have enjoyed their deaths," Sykar scoffed, taking a drink from his flask. We all had hip flasks filled with various spirits, like any self-respecting mysterious wanderer. Granted, while Sykar preferred rum, I always kept gin or slivovitz in mine. I never actually learned what the Night Witch had in hers, while Argus was the whiskey enjoyer of our group.

"Oh, gods no, never," I chortled. "I'll never get tired of replaying that moment in my mind! No, what I find myself worrying after is that one day I may come to miss that kind of power, and the privilege to call upon it against my foes. If that longing becomes desperation, who knows what I may create to scratch that itch again? Maybe it won't be the same as the Artifact, maybe it won't even be as powerful, but the principle will remain the same: Complete annihilation without the effort of skilled battle."

"I get what you're saying. I think if any of us were the ones to use it, we'd be thinking the same thing," the Night Witch commented. "The itch of retribution is not easily scratched correctly, but when it is... it does make you feel invincible. There are few better feelings than vengeance done *right*. But with vengeance done right comes the very real risk of complacency when you want to scratch that itch again, so eager and impatient that it doesn't get scratched right, and it doesn't feel the same."

"And when it's not the same, frustration is soon to follow," Sykar added. "Frustration that begets further impatience, and further failures to do it right. Nobody in the history of the darker path, ever walked that path from one act of vengeance. It always takes a second act... the one you do *wrong*."

I nodded and Argus took a longer drink out of his flask than normal. It seemed he had his fair share of brushes with vengeance done wrong, close calls where only last-minute instinct saved him and his honor, and gods only know how many unfortunate times when he had to put down those he once respected for it.

"It's hard to constantly muster the will to do it right," Argus commented, coughing a little as some drops of his drink took an extra second to go down, causing that very annoying sort of burn that you get when you put a little more than one swallow's worth in your mouth. "It's so disturbingly easy to decide *not* to take the extra step necessary to make sure, and yet it makes so much difference...."

The Night witch nodded, but then shook her head as she realized we had been melancholic about a great victory for too long now. "Let us not cloud the legitimacy of our victory with superstition and taboo," she declared. "We did it *right* today! Or rather, *Talon* did it right! We can either spend tonight unjustly somber about all the timelines in which we failed, or we can commemorate the fact that *ours* is the one where we succeeded! Celebration is not synonymous with complacency, so I say we celebrate, damn it!"

"She's right," I affirmed. "We *have* earned a victory here beyond all doubt! Though it was my boot that did the necessary deed afterwards, I have all of *you* to thank that I had the strength to do it. Today is a *good* day! Aurophile City is no more, and so too are its wretched inhabitants, the thieves of the masses and planet alike that no longer draw breath, and suffer forever in their worst afterlives!"

We all raised our flasks with an affirming, "Aye!" and took respectably sized drinks from them.

"Too bad we missed out on looting the place, though," Sykar cheekily added, and we all shared a chuckle at that. It didn't matter too much. If it meant that we missed out on the haul, we were all willing to leave it at the fact that Aurophile City, and its inhabitants, were no more.

"So, what's next for us?" I finally asked.

"We stay true to the Path: We continue wandering the world, we fix what's wrong, and we do what's right," the Night Witch affirmed. Everyone nodded and drank to that. It certainly could be said that between the four of us, we definitely liked being able to say, 'I'll drink to that,' and then proceeding to do so. Our vocation was such that though we lived with only the clothes on our backs, our skill and our unwavering morals had made those clothes, capes, and jackets the best versions of themselves they could be.

I find there is a difference between suspiciously well-armed brigands whose wealth is worn in terms of flashy symbols and sigils, and nomads who spend theirs instead on making their wardrobe the most practical and upgraded versions of themselves possible. There will never come a day when I feel intimidated by some militant carrying a bell-and-whistle enamored rifle in their hands, with pistols on each hip and another strapped across their chest, shotgun slung over their back and a belt of shells that the pistol's holsters are affixed to. When one person carries enough weapons to arm five, it is only a signal of their cowardice, their fear of fair fights and their sheer lack of skill, evinced by how many weapons they might drop, lose, or misuse to the point of breaking. Worry never about their skill, for they have none. I have yet to even take a single hit from one such sunshine soldier, and I can count on one hand how many have actually even been able to raise their weapons before my blades already were upon them. They *always* lack the conditioning to be able to carry all that steel with them for any longer than a few minutes before being completely out of breath, let alone trek across the hills, the plains, and the mountains.

With Aurophile City no more, we all agreed to walk our separate ways and meet up again in maybe a few hundred years, with new stories to tell each other of how the skulls of fascists were crushed by our hands. Where and when we would track each other down again, we did not know. All we knew was that this was neither goodbye nor farewell, but instead 'until next time.'

The perks of immortality are nigh uncountable, and many of them are just different ways of saying that there is great inner peace to be gained from knowing that you have time to match your ambitions, and that you never have to stop learning new things and collecting new skills, forging new stories and never having to worry about time's cruelty standing in your way.

When the dawn came, we each picked a direction. Four warriors, four cardinal directions. I chose north, while Argus took east. Sykar went south, and the Night Witch went forth west. Passing over the crater that was once the City of Greed and Jealousy, I left but one marker for history, so that when our world had been shaped by our honorable actions enough for warriors to hang their swords above their hearths and let gather dust, when archivists and archaeologists can once again be the wanderers instead of fighters and killers like us, this is what they will discover.

I Beheld Red Sparks

n amber cat's eyes
Became a shifting silver form in the blackness
Followed by a red spark on a burned sunset.

Prophecy? Pretension? Premonition? Madness? Meaninglessness? They are nigh indistinguishable if they are not one and the same.

Though by each second the words tried to slip away like the memory of a dream, I held onto them, burning them into my mind for so long as it might take for me to write them down. If I remembered to write them down, I would then attempt to draw the images that I beheld, which could only be described by those very words I was trying to ensure I remembered, out of a hope that if I could remember the words, I could remember the images, and so I could make them manifest in some form that could be recognized before they faded away entirely, for I did not trust my own mind to remember what needed be remembered.

Or perhaps those words and images needed no memory, and my mind was thus right in letting them slip away so quickly as they had come. But they seemed to demand to be clung to, in a way I could not understand why, for some reason, I could not help but think that these words, these images, had to mean something, even if that meaning was nothingness.

My head felt as though a drill were boring through my skull as I tried to cling to this lightning strike, demanding it stay with me for just a few moments longer, that I could wield it for even a few seconds, or at least learn how to.

Once I had done what I believed needed, penning the words and drawing the images as best as my hands could, I told myself I could let go, because this lightning had been wielded, and needed be hung onto no longer.

Why is it, I wonder, that such strangeness that seems only identical to meaningless rambling of a mind closer and closer to falling over the brink of insanity demands such attention from me? Why should I endeavor so fervently to hold on to that which presents no answers, but only seems to provoke cryptic questions alongside already cryptic ranting?

Are they the last fragments of reason that I dare hold on to, if only to remind those who may find these words in a more enlightened age what becomes of those like me?

Are they a grim prophecy promising doom, or benevolent premonition heralding prosperity?

I only know what the world would tell me today: *Madness, madness, madness, lock the madman up,* they would call. Would they be wrong? That I even must ask seems only to prove the answer.

I must ask myself alone these questions, for if I were to ask others, I would soon find myself behind bars, or worse: Within the walls of the insane asylum. Call them what you will in the tongue of today, but they remain the same, a sideshow for their workers to gawk at and to flex their power-hungry muscles on. But I digress.

An amber cat's eyes. Does this mean the mineral known as Cat's Eye? Does this mean the amber eyes of an actual cat? Does this mean the eyes of a cat whose fur is the color of amber? Or at least vaguely so? I feel as though this is honestly the easiest question of them all to answer, for the shifting silver form in the blackness is enigmatic to a nigh immeasurable degree.

Such is the problem with potential prophecy, is it not? Prophecy is a fickle beast, infinitely deniable as it is infinitely confirmable. This is why prophets are remembered long after their time, because their words can mean anything, for they understand vagueness and the fact that the masses are but sheep, ignorant fools who will gladly rally behind the invisible banner of an even more invisible commander. Replace banners with crosses and commanders with gods and they remain themselves all the same, non-entities who neither live nor breathe, purporting to demigodhood or godhood itself, demanding fear only as demons do, for the gods are ignorant rather than malicious. I will have their heads all the same, but once again, I digress.

Became a shifting silver form in the blackness. A shifting silver form appeared to take the shape of pseudo-shapes, a squarish ramp into an orb that would fly down it... but the orb just before landing upon the ramp took the shape of a human spleen and for this fact became unable to roll down the ramp. Ah yes, the spleen, the organ that loves to bleed. To headbutt someone with the disease known as Mononucleosis is to rupture this organ and result in internal bleeding unto death... a temptation I found myself having to resist when my sister contracted the disease. Perhaps I regret not taking the chance; I would have eliminated from my timeline an adolescent who, soon after, became entitlement-born toxicity made manifest, who believes herself above wrong in this day and age despite the crimes of her past. My hope remains that no soul could be foolish enough to fall in with an individual with still so much to answer for. But my vengeance mongering aside, I will save this debate for another day, when the lands are lawless and my enemies are within the scope of my rifle. On that day, I shall not hesitate, and I will only feel weight being lifted from my shoulders with the dropping to the ground of a lifeless corpse.

Followed by a red spark on a burned sunset. Even then, I understood well that the sunset was not burning, it was burned. Already had the fire passed, and the burnt orange hue signified such. *The sunset was already burned,* and these words seemed more important to me than any other, maybe even more so than the words of the three lines I made sure so hard to hang on to. The sunset was already burned... *already. Already. Already burned.* I feel filled with an overwhelming dread as I find that the sunset is *already* burned. But the red spark lay at the center, and the red spark fizzled and spun like the core of a ringularity, spinning and spinning with speed and energy beyond measure, crackling and sparking with the demand to be let loose, the demand to be seen and beheld, or at the very least, released from the confines of the sunset already burned.

Where lies the line between prose, pretension, and madness? I no longer care whether or not prophecy has a card to play, with the sunset burned and the silver form shifted, greyed away from the eyes that once could see, I only seek now to not be madness incarnate, insanity made flesh.

The eyes became a silver form, blasted away not by

the spark but by what burned the sunset. What burned the sunset? What brought the clouds to ruin, that saw them unable even to fall to the ground, but instead bleed the sky dry?

The spark promised neither recovery nor *coup de grace*, seemingly only content to remain a perpetual bringer of doubt and uncertainly to whether it would be what pulled prosperity from the jaws of ruin, or push all that is, was, and ever will be into the final darkness, swallowed by the void-touched maw of the Jormungandr. The form of silver could not have been the Serpent, however. This much I do know.

The sunset remained burned, and the silver form remained shifting, as the red spark fizzled in place, neither growing nor fading.

The fire of time.... The fire of time, ashes of madness on the winds of uncertainty. Decay promised by the fire and to extinguish it is only to bring entropy to its close prematurely? My answer is not in keeping the fire, nor diluting it, but in some new process, that means this fire can no longer burn that which it touches, or at least, myself, when it tries.

The spark is not indecisive. It has chosen not to decide, and yet it makes this known to none.

The shifting form of silver orbits erratically, seemingly against what the laws of physics should allow; it changes each time it cycles, as though trying to ensure that the spark remains undecided, despite its choice never to choose.

The amber eyes watch endlessly, warning of dire prophecy should the delicate dance falter, and yet... they become one another, one after the other, constantly looping in one process, over and over again, the eyes become the form, the form became the spark, and the sunset had been burned from the beginning.

The vision faded from me once again, and I was left wondering when it had even begun. Where was the line between reflection and re-manifestation? I somehow found myself unable to even think about trying to find out. An unearthly exhaustion overcame me, and yet I felt compelled to ward it off, by any way I could, though I did not understand why either side of that coin was vying for control over my next actions.

I tried to command myself to remember what I saw again, hoping that maybe in a revisit to this strange premonition, new details may reveal themselves that even if they could not give answers to my questions, perhaps they could at least lend a measure of credibility to them, solace in the knowledge that this was something more than nothing.

I remember that the amber cat's eyes were more like... a single eye with two pupils that seemed to bridge together towards their center with a strip of pure blackness flanked by eyes within them; it was as if within this one eye, there were two others, and a void between them as they looked to the left, and only leftwards, refusing to break its gaze upon what it could see, that I could not. I only knew that they would not blink in the face of whatever they were beholding, until they shifted into the silver form, and then the singular red spark.

I wish I understood why I felt the need to understand what became by the moment less akin to premonition and more likely pure madness, the last of my reason gasping its last before something new took hold, something that was not me. Was the prophecy then in that these were the signs that heralded my doom? Did the amber cat's eyes, the shifting silver form, and the red spark upon a burned sunset signal that my doom was to be upon me? If these images that could barely be discerned in my mind's eye became manifest in my life, were they the harbingers of my destruction? Or perhaps, did they signal its forthcoming in appearing before me in my prior contemplation?

Madness indeed, for if my life has become such that this is where my focus is spent, it truly must have gone so wrong, in so many ways that should never have been conceivable, let alone possible. If the standstill of progress that is my life's story is so hideously staunch and disturbingly immobile, that *this*, this gibberish of my mind is where I place my power in the name of decoding a cipher nonexistent…. But what else is there even to do?

Taking risks is banished from my willingness, for so many countless endeavors have crumbled the instant skill no longer had a say. It has always been the case, that the cemetery whose headstones read the ambitions and plans of my time, they all share one unifying cause of death: Luck was not on my side. If it were skill alone that dictated fortune, I would have been so much more, and now, as the voices of innumerable failures do naught but torment, and dreams only haunt, the only thing left it seems, is to let these ramblings of my mind, these unconnected images and words that I use to demand that I remember them, be where my thought is spent.

The sunset is burned, and only a red spark remains, flickering and dwindling in eternity, or at least, dragged out so long in its death throes that it may as well be. The silver form shifts and twists, as though trying to make something out of the nothingness. The amber cat's eyes look on, and though I know not whether they are the eyes that contemptuously and deliberately look away or affixed to some oncoming threat, all I know is that they are looking... *somewhere.* Somewhere else. Somewhere... else.

I can no longer see the eyes. The shifting silver form fades even now, try as I might to continue contorting it in my mind's eye, if only to ensure that it does not cease, by way of just not stopping. This is where my mind is spent? This is how my energy is expended? If the red spark is all that will remain, what will it be the remnant of?

Somehow, I get the feeling that question is already answered by the mere fact that I have spent so much time already debating to myself what any reasonable person would dismiss.

Am I the final bastion of reason in an era of madness? Am I its opposite, the last vestige of a school of thought long since proven wrong or worse? When I feel as though I am all that stands against the tidal wave of force against me, are those I see at my sides truly those who stand alongside me, who would gladly be as shoulder-to-shoulder as I would be, if only it were called upon? Are they the exemplars of evil brought themselves forth to indoctrinate me into their ranks? Will I discover a horrible truth about all I have known and admired, all that I have dared to value, that brings me nothing but shame for the fact that now my name is among theirs?

Which hills are the worthy ones to declare that I shall die upon? Where are the hills that will see my name remembered like the exemplars of evil I once swore to destroy? How do I find out, which one is which? Who could I trust to tell me? Must I rely solely on myself to say? How will I tell the difference between who to trust, who to take up arms against for their place among the sea of troubles, who will stand beside me in opposition to end them? Who will bring me to my hands and feet when I fall to my knees, to tell me that today is not my final day, and that to die and to sleep, is to only allow their accursed feet to trample upon the land and bring a plague of death and dishonor upon the grass that I once loved to tread upon?

Who will it be, if not me?

When will it be, if not now?

Is it my right to bear this burden? Is it my place to defer it? All I know today is that I wish only to bring death to those whose evils made it my duty to ask.

May Flame Await
the Luck-Blessed

Grateful as I was to finally get my legs out the door and walking, wandering to *somewhere*, the scale at which the point was missed was infuriating. They acted like this meant that it worked, when all it showed was just how much it *didn't*. That it took the grace of chance just to find fulfillment showed how vile and broken the world around me had become.

I first received the letter of selection on a rainy day, the skies as grey as my future. People sometimes say that listening to the rain fall is satisfying. I disagree. The sound is a reminder of what awaits you should you dare to step outside when the world so devoutly stands against you: The downpour of an unholy will to stop your ambitions. The last bastion I may be, but the bastion's walls are old and tired, as is its single occupant.

Regardless, the form-letter of formally-worded correspondence spared no shortage of congratulatory flair and praise for how lucky I was to be selected for the Explorer's Corps, Sea Division. Fleet Nine, Submarine Six. I'm not even sure if the vessel I'm to serve on has a name, to be honest. Though I could not deny that I was presented with an opportunity I would be a fool to ignore, I could not ignore that *this*—this random chance—was what decided I could prosper now, instead of skill. If it were skill alone that dictated fortune, I would have been so much more.

They claim they made the world better. They did not.

They claim they made it all equal. They did not.

They claim lies to their credit, and act like heroes when they bless some random citizen with the life they should have been able to live in the first place, and act like it's a privilege when instead it is a right.

They claim vindication of all their words and all their teachings, and that this wheel of fortune is demonstration of how well their system works, when it proves the opposite. No one should have to beat incredible odds just to live decently, and *that* was what they created. Crowds of cowards insist that it works, mindless mongrels and people with less brain cells than teeth have come under the impression that this insult to life itself is a good thing, and the only hope I have is that they will not be spared. Neither cruelty nor coward can be allowed to live in the end.

If it means that flame must await me, too, then so be it. History will not remember me as a hypocrite. I will not consider myself exempt from the rule of 'Fuck Them' if it applies to me.

...

I have grown so tired of only dreaming of vengeance and retribution. The opportunity presented to me promises solace, but I can only see all the reasons that it means the system *doesn't* work. Mine is not a tale of the value of perseverance, nor a testament to the benefits of what they created. It is the opposite.

When I received the letter saturated with honeyed words and formal praises, inviting me to partake in the grand privilege of prosperity and fulfillment, all I could think was that this letter would have come to me regardless of how hard I tried. All the clawing I had done until now may as well have been spent doing nothing if the reward is all the same, granted only by chance, rather than by merit.

Have I grown so bitter—and vengeful for it—that my memory falters, too? Have I already groused endlessly of this yet have failed to recall it? The days grind on all the same, chipping away bit by bit what is left of me.

Have I even the strength left to answer the call? Has my strength left me? Was there any to begin with? I feel as though I have asked these questions before but I cannot remember if I have. This seems like only further proof of my decay, if so.

But all that said, I now had a chance. Not everyone has the strength to set the world on fire.

The time for self-pity has passed. Now is the time for steel.

The induction ceremony spared no expense, like the bribe that it was, hoping to stop me from what I knew I had to do. I was told to bring only what I needed, and so I brought my sword. I needed only await the moment of destiny.

The host of the event, the figurehead of a grey regime decorated in stars unearned, addressed the crowd. But his microphone wasn't working. The speakers that were supposed to be relaying his honeyed speech weren't connected to his pulpit. As a sound team wondered what was going on, so did I. This wasn't part of my plan. I was just going to stab him once I got within six feet….

Suddenly, drums and distorted guitar riffs began to pump through the speakers and I recognized the song. It was a song of battle, a rallying cry to take up arms and do what was right.

The gate that kept the riff-raff from the event was suddenly blown down as the music picked up and I knew that the moment of destiny had come. I pulled my blade from its sheath and ran the old bastard at the pulpit through, kicking him off the stage just as the confused guards froze for one deciding moment in the confusion. The others who were with me—similar winners of the explorer's hat-draw—were even more so baffled. They couldn't tell if they should join me or destroy me for the merit of it.

Four shots rang out and cut down the guards that had just raised their weapons at me. The audience that had gathered—loyal sheep of the system—scattered in a chorus of screams and confused yelling.

From the dust of the destroyed gate, I saw four warriors, armed and armored, walking towards me. How, I didn't know but I *knew*, somehow, I just *knew* that these three men and one woman were the kind of people that when they showed up, you fought beside them.

I shoulder-checked one of the un-indoctrinated off the stage as he grabbed the rifle of his superior. He'd perhaps been hoping to quickly kill one of the assailants, to earn good faith with people who couldn't give less of a shit about him than if they went on a four-day camping trip, had no bowel movements as a stress response, and ended up with an intestinal blockage. The warriors who had just crashed the ceremony all pulled arms and began fighting the grey guardsmen of the regime that they had come to end and I would be damned if I did not fight beside them.

So I did.

With nothing left to lose, I decided that if this was my final day, in this first and last battle, I would not go quietly, nor would I go without some impressive feats to my name. With the spirit of battle setting my veins ablaze to the tune of the ballads that rang through the air, from the speakers that these warriors four had commandeered, I swung my heel at the next of the Greyguards who approached; he never saw the wheel kick coming. He likely was counting on my submission; instead, he met my fury. His head slammed against the raised platform intended to host the indoctrination of dozens of disciples set to worship a decrepit and corrupt system. But now, it was *my* stage, my arena where I made tyrants and cowards alike kneel to the metal of my sword and obligingly cease living.

As I cut down the men who crossed my way, I could see glimpses of the warriors four during their displays of martial prowess, watching one slice a leg from his opponent, only to grab the detached limb and hurl it at another foe, slamming the boot into their face and dropping the scoundrel to the ground.

The songs of battle continued to pump through the speakers, the anthems and drums that inspired the valorous and signaled the doom of the iniquitous. I found myself lost in a trance of combat, my eyes only saw what needed be seen— which opponents needed be skewered or sliced next—and where they were vulnerable. I saw where to parry, where to duck and dodge, where to strike.

How many foes we felled, I do not know. The kinds of

people who count their kills never live long enough to brag about it, anyway.

The sun set over a decimated den of evil. We were victorious. Then, for the first time, I heard one of the warriors speak.

"It's been… a long time since I've seen someone *new* fight like that," one of the men said as he sheathed his sword and collected one of his revolvers dropped during the battle.

I did not reply as the other three gathered to meet me, still standing on the stage that, before they showed up, would have commemorated my capitulation to foes who made fulfillment a privilege. Instead, it was now their gravestone.

"We had best get moving, Sykar," the woman informed. "The city's about to collapse in on itself. You might want to travel with us for now, at least."

I realized she had suddenly turned to inform me of this so I followed the four out of the city, looking back upon the gates that I once thought kept me safe, but that now I knew did nothing but bind me to a cruel and trapped fate.

I grabbed a stone from the ground and threw it at the wall in defiance, for what it was worth; I left to explore the world on my *own* terms, rather than this city's.

"It's been quite a while since we've seen anyone stand out in a crowd like that," one of the warriors commented after he set up a fire for us all to gather and reflect on the day around. "It's… a relief, honestly."

I had yet to say a word to any of them, still. The one that the woman referred to as Sykar spoke next.

"Normally, there are two kinds of people in these cities: The ones doing the oppressing and the ones who praise their overlords from it. The so-called 'rebels' only appear once the power vacuum is made, and they're hardly bastions of defiance as much as opportunistic bootlickers," he said. "But once in a blue moon, there's a couple of people who *aren't* that. People who never let themselves be convinced that it's right for such wretchedness who stand, and who despise every moment that they are surrounded constantly by cowards."

"Of course, there's always the question: What makes them any different, if they too waited until the day of destiny to finally do what they knew was right all along?" the woman continued. "But there's no inherent dishonor in general self-preservation; there's wisdom to be had in knowing that striking now will only grant you an empty death and a villainous legacy."

I sat in silence, having just been asking myself that very question after Sykar said his piece.

"Maybe it is in survival that the question is answered. Maybe it is in what one does *after* survival that does it," the other man whose name I did not know yet said. "It never seems to have a solid answer, that question. What I do know is that it's quite obvious that you wanted to do what you did today for a *very* long time. Perhaps a whole lifetime."

Finally, I spoke: "Maybe *that* is what decides who is who in the fray. Or more likely, it discerns who may be the worst of the lot."

"Maybe it presents a new dilemma between those two. Maybe whichever one of that you turn out to be presents itself *another* one. The cycle of dilemmas refuses to cease." Sykar grunted. "It's annoying as hell that answers seem forbidden."

I sighed in agreement. "It does seem very annoying. Granted, I'm rather new at this whole independence thing, so you'll have to forgive me if I'm a little slow at first."

"Good gods, this one reminds me of myself when I first got started!" Sykar returned. "Slow? Your choice to break the chains was anything *but* slow! You cannot be blamed for waiting until your opportune moment to make your stand but you didn't freeze when the time was nigh and *that* makes all the difference, I think."

"It at least means that you've got promise. Promise that you now have a chance that you had previously been denied the opportunity to see through until today."

Suddenly, I realized that I recognized the woman's hat. I just hadn't put it together yet because... because the Night Witch, Sykar the Lightningclaw, the Talon of the Sea, and Argus Steelheart were all ancient history!

"History says that you all disappeared seven hundred years ago, after you destroyed the great bastion of darkness, Aurophile City!" I said suddenly. "How—"

"Seven hundred twenty-two, actually," Argus corrected.

"You were counting?" Talon scoffed.

"Someone had to be," Argus countered.

"After Aurophile was destroyed, our work was pretty much done," the Night Witch recalled. "It was this great, golden abomination that contained every single son-of-a-bitch on the planet who *liked* the idea of that kind of city and everything it stood for. The rest were scattered and disorganized after we had turned their center of power to dust."

"We hung up our weapons and called it a day, figuring

that if we were needed again, we could dust them off and get back to doing what we do best," Argus continued.

"About seventy years ago, rumors began circling, whispers of a newly found nostalgia for the greed that was that city," Sykar followed up. "We prepared to move out again to deal with it. Twenty years later, the city you just helped us torch was finished, and its doors closed."

"And you waited this long to act?!" I demanded.

"When he says the doors closed, he means in a metaphorical sense," the Night Witch corrected. "The city had *just* been built. It was the new Aurophile, and if we bulldozed it immediately, the prey would scatter. We had to wait until we knew that everyone who had a stake in that way of life was there, and could be snuffed out all at once."

I still wasn't having any of it. "So how many people like me lived and died while you waited?!"

"Too damn many, I would imagine," Argus solemnly noted. "It wasn't an easy decision to make. Move in now, kill only *some* of the enemy, but save the people like you? Or wait until we could kill *all* of the enemy, knowing that this very conundrum would be our reward."

"Not everyone has the strength to set the world on fire, fewer still have the strength to wait until they know it'll burn the right targets to ashes," the Night Witch concluded. "The lifetime you lived until today is inexcusable, there can be no doubt. But I hope I speak for both of us when I say there's no point in dwelling on that now; yes, you've not only walked out of that gate for the first time now, but you left behind a ruined bastion of evil that *you helped* bring to fall."

I contemplated her words. She wasn't wrong, but it still didn't feel right. I think that mostly, it had to do with the sheer anger and disgust I felt that people had become *nostalgic* for Aurophile City. They took one look at what that bastion of evil was—the wretched iniquity that radiated from it, and the broken morals it needed to function—and they thought: *I'd like to see that again...* even with the hindsight of history on their side. It just made it worse. Shaky as the argument is that the people might not have known better, there *is* no excuse for wanting to bring it back.

"Every now and again, people like us need reminding what we're here for," Talon reflected. "It seems the time for us to wander the world and set it right has come once more. But today, we've been shown that we need not number only four—if you would wish to join us on our immortal quest for justice and reason."

My chance had come, and not by luck this time. By the steel of my sword and the strength of my arm, I had broken the chains of the Grey Citadel that was my home, and by steel and skill, I had earned the right to wander.

That was something I could do.

Solace Only
in Solitude

have quite the fondness for winter. I despise summer, and spring simply has too much rain. As for autumn... I'm sure I could enjoy it more if not for the magnet of pretension it bears the unenviable role of. How many vomit-inducing, sappy poems are named "Autumn Leafs" or "Autumn's Grace" and similar, I shudder to think of, for I have no doubt the number is harrowingly high.

Winter knows no such deception as spring, luring you out the door with promises of sunshine, to only dash them with the bitterness of pouring rain. It also knows no such draining beatdown from the sun as summer, and though winter has its own share of pretentious louts who couldn't tell the difference between poetry and just looking up every word in a thesaurus droning on about a beauty I prefer to appreciate in person and in silence instead of gushing on about, I suppose every season has them, but I think autumn got the worst of the lot, and the most. A pity.

I am no beacon of misery, no lover of suffering. That would be my mother, but that's beside the point. I do not find joy in demanding that expressions cease and that every hand be scrutinized before the privilege of picking up a pen. But I do prefer to spend what time I can beholding the serenity of vistas alone, in silence, and without the nagging annoyance that is the drive to write about it, or reach for my smartphone to take a picture, like I prioritize the picture over what is being captured. I would say that the pictures are for the second visit. The memoirs are for when you are beyond the moment, and no longer caught up in how you'll write about it, or how quickly you can draw your phone from your pocket to take pictures obsessively.

Am I insane or am I the last of the sane? I doubt I'll ever know. I only know what others would say. Only in solitude and silence have I ever found solace. Winter, the essence of silent solitude. In the stillness I have found strength, and in the biting winds I have found the way to hone it, sharpen it, that my hands may be as tough as the tundra permafrost, of tundra and mountains I long to return to.

Where are the mountains I was promised I would climb?

Where are the paths I dreamed of walking? Why has the eternal search led to nothing, not even the search itself?

More importantly, who is responsible, that I can make suffer for what they stole from me?

As much as I grow weary of my lust for vengeance, what else is there to dream of in this grey century?

I only dream of retribution, punishment, vengeance, payback....

I'm almost gone, aren't I?

Someday, someone will look at these words, and they will say, with the hindsight of history, the future I am doomed to never see... what will they say? When they see these words, what vindication of their woes will I confirm?

What shameful break of my mind that has yet to come, do they reflect on that is their history? With no end to the madness in sight, and with more and more people than ever suspecting my insanity… who will make the mistake of drawing first blood? Who will bear the venerated role of their defense, against the unjust aggressor? Who will they who look upon these words in the future scorn, and rightfully so?

It seems that the winter has given me the grace of this insight, as winter itself becomes rarer and rarer in the Grey Century. Here where I dream of bringing the deserved fate upon the wicked, only to dream of it. All the sleepless nights where I let my mind wander, gone are their visions of distant worlds and bright glories in victory alongside warrior allies, kindred in spirit. Gone are the names of the brave and the bold, replaced only by the wishful thinking of all the ways I would teach the heralds of the Grey Century the meaning of pain.

Even if one day the cowardice of the masses is replaced by the will of valor that is so infuriatingly absent, my grand dread is that it is so far beyond my time, that it may as well not even exist, for no method will ever exist that will allow me to see it. The future may as well not exist, because it does not for me.

The heralds of the Grey Century have not even the decency to exile themselves to an isle of decadence, where at least they would be away from the rest of the world, but instead see only the need to ensure that everyone else knows where they are, and that they are there. I dream only of their severed heads adorning a field of stakes that stretches into the horizon, and the most painful ways of severing them that mortal hands can inflict. I dream of their agony, their frozen expressions of terror and pain, and nothing else.

Why are most people cowards? Why, damn it.... I dream of their heads on pikes, too, you know. I will not be ashamed to admit it, that after the heads of the heralds adorn the fields, I will wish the cowards' heads next. If they have no will to defend, then let them know pain everlasting, for lying on their backs and submitting themselves to the whims of the heralds of the Grey Century.

Will I be all that is left after the crusade is done? Perhaps it will be for the best that none remain.... Perhaps my final victory will be that I will be the final darkness cleansed. The greatest victory, that none can know of.

I dread not this fate. Instead, the fate where this is the only one left for me, and that my chance, my opportunity, my path does not evade me for so long that this is the only thing left I can see.

Sometimes, I can remember the distant worlds, and the bright glories. Flashes of light in the dark that illuminate the room, and give me but the blink of an eye's time to commit as much as I can to memory.

But this is what has become of me, has it not? I started this prose with making known my fondness of winter, and now, here I am again, confessing over and over my lust for vengeance, and my dreams of when the time of retaliation finally comes. But this is what becomes of men like me when the mountains are stolen, when the paths are blocked, and opportunity becomes as fictional as prosperity. My fondness of winter stands next to my dreams of vengeance, because those dreams take up so much space—almost all of it— bringing the distant worlds and the bright glories into the dark corners where the dreams of vengeance should be instead.

The winter I found myself so fond of, the solace in solitude that I dread, will forever be fiction.... I wish I could place my thoughts to ends other than retribution. I wish I still had the will to dream of the distant worlds. But my enemies surround me, and my allies do not exist. Who would have me, anyway? I wouldn't have me, and for good reason, too.

Perhaps the winter will have me.

Let my bones become as hardened as the rock of the mountains, let my skin become as the toughest packed snow upon them. Let my mind become as sharp as the bite of the frozen winds, and let my will become as unmoving as the mountains I will stand atop. If I am so denied the mountains, then I will become them, and my wrath shall be as the glacial rivers that rage upon the thieves who stole the mountains.

I will carry each rock on my shoulders to place them where they belong until the mountains are rebuilt, and my frozen heart shall bring the winter whose solitude will bring me solace. If this is what must be done, so be it, because no one else will.

Because no one else will.... What will I become at the end of the endeavor? As those five words may bring me the spite-born motivation to see it through, they may also infest my mind with the bitterness-born greed that will see me deny all others what I have reclaimed, because I had to do it myself, because no one else would. Where is the line that I must not cross? What is the decision that will place me on one side or the other? Spite and bitterness I define separately, but the line that separates them is thin, and the threshold all but invisible in the heat of the moment. What form will that moment take? What will I behold, that means that the moment is nigh?

Where the path splits, and time dictates that events shall be one of two, and no in-between… what, or who, will herald this split?

Yet even in this pondering, there is no solace so long as the winter remains stolen, and stolen it remains. Am I preparing myself for this eventuality or am I passing by opportunity after opportunity to make things right as I remain so focused on the questions of what and when? Does it aid me to think this or does it doom me to do so? Is every question a wasted chance?

At this point, it must not be. Lest I have forfeited a dozen lifetimes' worth of rectification and the means to bring it about, all because it was based on chance. Chance, the rival and enemy of mine that ensures my stagnation, for chance refuses to be in my favor, and when chance is permitted any due, *that* is when it all goes wrong.

It must not be chance alone. It should not be chance alone. And yet… the Grey Century demands chance be in your favor; but it isn't chance, is it? No, they just *say* that it is chance to cover for the fact they have killed chance itself and replaced it with the walls that keep the mountains and the winter in their grasp and away from us all—not out of any desire to protect them but only the desire to deprive us of them, to say that only *they* can have the mountains, only *they* can have the winter.

Make no mistake: What is lost to them is what they have stolen, and there can be no sin in ripping their hands from their wrists in the name of reclaiming what belongs to no one, *especially* not *them*.

You know of whom I speak, for their names are written all around you.

You see them every day and learn of their lavish lives against your will.

They who deserve nothing, for they have stolen everything.

Even solitude itself is stolen by them, for your lives are infested by their unholy will to clog every grapevine, every newsfeed, demanding every ear be open to their gossip and dross.

And yet, all that I have seen is that this is what you wanted. If anything else were true, things would be different.

Is it any wonder I seek solitude in the cold winter? The frigid reaches were no one else dares follow?

If nothing else, if I were to take back the mountains and the dark wills see me too far gone to return them, you at least would never hear my name again, disappeared into the solitude and solace within, and if nothing else, I will no longer need suffer your cowardice and submission.

But that I even consider it seems to show that this may very well be the less than honorable path I take; but what else can be done when all others have none of their own? Why allow the spineless masses what they were deprived of yet had no will to reclaim? Why should I share in what I took back from the enemy, when *I* was the one who had to do it?

A few years ago, this debate would not have existed in my mind. I would have only known and understood that I would reclaim life for all life. But now, here I am, considering refusal as punishment for the cowardice of the masses.

If anything else were true, things would be different.

What I would give to be able to do absolutely everything myself, to need nothing of anyone else, to need no one else for anything; if I were shown a way that, if I took it, meant I would never need to ask another person for anything again, that I would never need to rely on another person to any extent, I would take it. I would take it without hesitation; I would take it without regret and not a day would pass in a billion lifetimes that I regretted the sheer boon of pure and true independence.

Perhaps the winter will have me, so that no one has to suffer me. Perhaps the winter will have me, so that I need not suffer anyone else.

But first, I must reclaim the winter, and I must reclaim the mountains. I must bring to fall the hands that stole them from us all. I must carve them to cutlets and bring exquisite death upon them. I must bring the vengeance and retribution I dream of, if only to silence them from my mind and let them rest in their fulfillment. I only hope that the day comes before it is too late for me to learn who I will be once I have found that which I seek.

Perhaps the winter will have me, so that I may find these answers in the solitude I long for—that I need, that I dream of—in the few moments when my dreams are of things other than what I would do to those who stole the winter, the mountains, the paths to and among them.... Needless greed should be met with violence done upon its committers to match. If that must be me, then so be it.

And once the winter is reclaimed and the mountains are mine to wander, perhaps they will have me, not because I unchained them from the decrepit hands of the undeserving but because it will mean that none can follow me, whether to avenge someone I brought a deserved death to, or to thank me for what I will have done. Neither should have to endure my bitterness; a bitterness that I dread will remain long after the deeds I dream of are done.

The time for my dreams beyond vengeance, it seems, is over for now. What few streaks of light shone through the cracked stone has faded, and the wellspring of bloodlust flows again, demanding the blood of the guilty.

Perhaps when the winter has me, that wellspring will be frozen, and the world shall be better off for it.

An Ode to the Augment

When I first comprehended the weakness of my flesh... it disgusted me.

May my bones be replaced with metal unbreaking.

May my organs be swapped with their betters.

Let my blood become, instead, an unspoiling oil that ensures my chains are broken.

May the chains that bind me to mortality's contempt be shattered, the sharp shrapnel tearing my foes asunder.

Let the mockery of the gods cease forever that I was granted more ambition than time.

That now, I may mock them with my freedom from their whim, from the whim, the rust of entropy's evil grasp.

Let my skin become hardened as leather, unbruising when struck by mace and flail alike.

Let my muscle be denser than any mortal man's, to the point that no blade can cleave through my limbs.

Let my bones be as steel, as titanium, as tungsten, unbreaking as my will shall match.

That which was breakable, remade into unbreaking, and beyond what man's weapons can damage.

That which would break off, replaced in mere minutes, regenerated with speed that ensures no wound shall slay me.

Let this be my body as my mind remains, my consciousness the same as it has been through the years.

The years before, and that which will come after, unmoving are my morals and my mind, my self.

And time becomes no longer a foe of mine, unable to enact its whim of rust and decay.

Though not indestructibly eternal, but not so fragile and mortal, upgraded, evolved, optimized.

May my body be as steel as my mind, my bones as unbreakable as my will.

Let the contempt of decay be itself defied, that no longer I am cursed with more ambition than time.

Let bolt, gear, and wire bring my eyes to their peak, able to see and tell me what must be observed. Their vision sharper than a titanium blade, thus my vision as clear as the cloudless sky.

Let pin and rivet make my joints know no creak, render lift, rotation, and strain inconsequential.

By wire and gear may my ears hear all, yet able to discern and filter until what must be heard is observed. No foe shall be able to approach unnoticed, by Augment I become impossible to sneak up on.

May the speed of the Machine be sewn into my very form, its strength to match with the instincts I forged.

May flesh's weakness be purged, and its strengths preserved, that I become the living nightmare of my foes.

Countless fools will call me cursed, but they are ignorant, they are fools, they would gladly march towards empty death if their overlords demanded it. Their words will be as meaningless as the weakness I left behind, and will serve just as much purpose.

Whether for envy or because they were told to and possess no minds of their own, they will cry cursed, they will cry abomination, they will screech and they will wail.

They are welcome to fail to destroy me, and their bones will become the dirt I walk upon.

They are welcome to scream themselves to death, their throats cracked and tongues dried, that they knew no purpose but reckless, senseless evil and hate.

They are welcome to die as emptily as they deserve, while thanking the next on my list for the honor of the worms.

They are welcome to crumble as they giggle in their ignorance, as their bodies betray them, becoming dust in the wind, and as nameless as the dust.

They are welcome to succumb to terror as they realize what fools they were, and that their souls belong to the Nidhogg all the same.

We shall see who is cursed then.

When I first comprehended the weakness of my flesh... *it disgusted me.*

These words echoed endlessly in my head as I repeated them in preparation for the inevitable flow of anesthetic gas that would ensure my unconsciousness through the operation. The technology was experimental in name alone; the chance of failure was less than one percent. The eagerness with which I volunteered myself for this program initially made me wonder if it was worrying the higher-ups, but now I think they were just glad to have a volunteer, zeal was but a bonus to them. My ode to augments was the last thing on my mind as I drifted off into the sleep of surgery, the last time I would ever be under the knife. Not because these were my last moments, but because the weaknesses that plagued my body were being dealt with, permanently. My dreams of no longer being a prisoner of my own flesh were coming true, and so long as that less than one percent chance of failure remained unmanifested, I would suffer disease and defect no more.

When I first comprehended the weakness of my flesh... it disgusted me.

I thought I would awaken to the steady beeping of a heart rate monitor, but I did not. There was no IV needle in my arm, nor any monitoring machines hooked up to me. I felt as though all strength had left my arms, for I could not lift them. But this was to be expected, they said. That it would take some time before my body had adjusted to its upgrade. Minutes passed, and I finally was able to lift my arm, and myself, up in the bed I was laying on. But something about this bed was... different. It seemed to be made of something far more sturdy than the aluminum frame one might come to expect from a hospital bed.

"Morning, Captain Sykar," the attending nurse addressed me once he'd noticed I'd awakened.

"The others?" I managed to ask.

"A rousing success for all four of you. If I didn't know better, I'd say that *because* you four were so excited to get all that tech in your bodies, that's why it went so well." A moment passed as he processed what he had just said. "Eh, now that I think about it, there's probably some mind-over-matter stuff to it. Either way, congratulations. The 'weakness of your flesh' as you constantly put it, has been left behind."

I looked at my arm. There was still regular skin on it; I could feel it. That, and the muscle beneath. The weaknesses had been left behind indeed, and it seemed that their strengths would be preserved. Strengths such as being passable as a human person to the casual observer.

"Of course, we had to design new steel beds for you lot. I also don't think you'll be allowed on passenger flights anymore.... I'd also recommend staying out of old, dilapidated buildings. You've added quite a few pounds to yourself. But the trade-off is that it's all mechanical muscle."

"Is the Colonel around?" I asked. "I'd rather talk to him than a nurse."

He nodded, saying that he would let him know I was awake. He seemed to understand my aversion to nurses; any nurse claiming to be one of the good ones would. And I still would not believe them... though the 'good' ones would understand why.

As I did my best to gather my bearings and move around without straining myself in this fresh, new-and-improved body of mine, another man walked through the door.

"Your three friends all woke up before you, Captain," he said in a lighthearted tone. "I'd say they've been worried sick that you were the one who'd die under the knife, but they know better than to worry about you."

"And I know them too well to believe they'd ever insult me with their worry," I said as I shifted into a sitting position. Things seemed to be adjusting with more haste now; it would only be a matter of time before my strength would be at its full potential, a potential light-years beyond mere mortal men.

"Of course, there's no way to tell if the anti-aging stuff worked for about ten years or so, but I figure that's the least of anyone's concerns."

"Is there a concern?" I asked. "It sounds like it all went perfectly."

"If I were a more paranoid man, I'd say it went *too* perfectly. A quartet of misfits with distinguished service records who had already been buddies since high school, all eagerly volunteering for Project Tungsten? And to top it off, *all four* of them go under the knife without a hitch? It seems... so damned storybook."

"The way I see it, Colonel, it's a pretty good story so far. Where'd you put my uniform, anyway? I've always hated hospital gowns...."

"They've got it at the front desk; we'll walk there."

"Sounds good to me," I said as I finally stood up, planting my feet on the floor. I noticed some small cracks in the laminate from when I hopped off the bed. "Hm... I'll have to re-tool my kinesthetic awareness."

"That's almost word-for-word what Lieutenant Argus said."

Colonel Vlandeer seemed oddly determined to get some idle chatter in with me as we walked towards the nearby admin desk. He wasn't one for small talk, and that's why we always got along so well. His sudden talkativeness made me uneasy for reasons I could not pinpoint.

Soon, myself and my three closest friends met up at a nearby bar once we had all been cleared for release.

"Heyo, Sykar," one of them greeted. She was only

nicknamed the Night Witch by our enemies, because her great-grandmother was one of them who defected to the UK just before the construction of the Berlin Wall. It took a long time before 'Night Witch' had replaced her normal call-sign: 'Tube.' She'd claimed that one following an incident in Basic, a failed hazing attempt that saw thirteen recruits in the hospital at the end of an aluminum tube. "There are, like, seven under-covers here who are assigned to tail us." She was a very all-business person. I never minded.

"To watch, protect, or kill?" I asked.

"Definitely not protect," another one of my compatriots weighed in as he sat down at the circular booth to join us. During a joint exercise with some Greek special forces, he had earned the nickname 'Argus.' He still refuses to explain why. Insists that it would 'ruin the surprise.' Given that he was not one to shy away from discussing his combats, we can only guess who he had to impress, and with what.

"I hate being watched," I commented.

"We all do. How do we lose 'em, you figure?" The last of our quartet of misfits wondered aloud as he sat down with us. With the strange fortune of having the surname of 'Talon,' and his conscious competency to *not* humiliate himself during his first few months on base, he'd somehow gotten that name to stick.

"I get the feeling we won't have to. They may just be here to kill us," I noted, as I had noticed that the under-covers were actually doing quite a terrible job at being covert. They kept looking over at us then staring under their tables to undoubtedly send texts to their superiors. "Though... I don't think they're working together. Something tells me that there's seven people, each from different agencies, all with one mission. Or… maybe seven different agencies are all collaborating to kill us or competing for the right to," I postulated.

"It'd give us an excuse to see if Project Tungsten is all its cracked up to be… or if we've just gained a few hundred pounds in the form of metal skeletons," Argus said, almost eager to get stated.

"Well, let's let them make the mistake of the first move," Talon advised, to no argument.

The night continued as we started to figure out that the augments we had been so eager to get had also made us pretty damn hard to inebriate. With my enhanced ears, I could hear the conversation between server and barkeep:

"Do we cut them off? That's like… their twelfth round."

"I don't know; they don't even look buzzed to me."

"How is that even possible?"

"No idea but it looks like that's what they're doing."

I was just glad that our drinks and food were paid for by the program.

"The Bulgarian one is being told to make his move as soon as he walks out," Argus informed. "I could hear the phone conversation; that's gonna take some getting used to."

"I just heard the Russian be told over the phone to stop bothering with watching us and try to infiltrate the hospital," the Night Witch reported.

"The other five at that table are apparently a collaborative effort by several Arab League countries, and they're gonna try to off us once we leave," Talon added.

"Well, if we all leave at the same time, everyone's gonna expose themselves trying to make their moves simultaneously.... Let's leave when the Russian does, to get to the hospital," I suggested. We all figured it was a solid plan.

As soon as he stood up, the four of us did as well. This was immediately followed by *everyone* who'd we'd identified as watching us standing up. The whole room froze as we all realized the simultaneous actions. You could hear a pin drop as we looked to our adversaries and they all realized just how many people were interested in us.

The Russian suddenly reached for a gun in his coat but the Bulgarian jumped over a table to tackle him to the ground as we made our exit, tailed by the remaining five players in this equation.

As soon as we were out of the bar, we had to decide whether or not to use these new augments of ours to decimate our pursuers or evade them with inhuman efficiency.

There was no need for words; we were all in silent agreement.

Five dead attackers later, we could only wonder what was going on inside, as only a few people had run out the door, and no shots were heard. We could only figure that the Bulgarian had subdued the Russian successfully, and that he would just rest on the laurels of stopping a shooting.

A black van pulled up to us and the window rolled down as Colonel Vlandeer told us to get inside, and quickly. We might as well, was the next silent agreement between our quartet of misfits.

"What in all the fucking bullshit was *that?!*" I demanded to know. "And why weren't we made aware that—"

"Stop talking, Sykar," Colonel Vlandeer ordered. The

odd feeling of wrongness from before was only stronger now. "A lot of people are competing for the right to kill you four, and there are bounties in over a dozen countries for your heads."

"What? Just because we volunteered to become stronger?!" Argus piped up. "Or because it *worked?!*"

"Because it worked, damn it!" Vlandeer yelled again. "What is it with you four and questioning absolutely everything?!"

As the argument continued, I couldn't ignore the pounding warning in my head, the unease that started just after the operation was successful. My instincts, trained by flesh and now honed by steel, told me that this man was *not* our ally.

"It's too much for one day... too damn much, it's all happening at once," I processed aloud.

"I thought I told you to stop talking!"

Then I remembered the reason *why* I had even suspected Vlandeer in the first place. Where the unease started, in the hospital, but *not* after the operation. I saw him reading a book as we were led into the place, before we were formally introduced. I remembered now which book it was.

Several extra hundred pounds of metal enhancing every part of my body was going to need to be used again, as now the Night Witch began to suspect Vlandeer as well when he missed the turn to the hospital.

The weakness of flesh would not have survived the ensuing wreck. The weakness of the late Colonel's certainly didn't. But we did, all four of us, with at most bruises and scrapes. Not even a cracked rib.

As I helped Argus out of the ditch our overturned

vehicle had found itself in following multiple rolls, I reassured my friends: "If nothing else, we can blame the Colonel's death on one of the dozen or so countries that want our heads."

"I can't help but feel like we're standing in one of them," Talon noted.

As much as we needed to find the time to process this all, we also needed to get the hell out of dodge, and to a hiding place. Fortunately, the trees that surrounded the highway provided plenty of space for us to lose any followers in, and the enhanced stamina of our augments meant we could sprint for hours without even breaking a sweat.

Once we were confident that the cover of darkness had fully ensured our escape, we all stopped and took a breather, though none of us were tired.

"I'm not winded, not even a little bit," Argus noted with quiet impress.

"Seems the operation worked. We've truly left the weakness of flesh behind," I stated.

Sirens and shouts could be heard but even dozens of miles away, we could hear them.

"I'm going to have to learn to control that better..." I said. "I don't much like the idea of being able to hear sirens all day long, just because they're blaring somewhere."

"I mean, think about it. This is quite literally the loudest era of all history. There's never been so much damn *noise* before," Argus pointed out.

"So what do we do now?" the Night Witch asked, seemingly determined to make sure we addressed that before any other more introspective or philosophical conversations could take place. "The world hunts us, whether to kill or weaponize what we've finally become."

"We'll have to split our paths here, I think," Talon suggested. "There are four of us, so we'll choose a cardinal direction each and just... go. If we truly have left the weakness of flesh behind, we'll live long enough to come back to this spot and meet up again."

None of us were too fond of the idea, but we all knew it was likely necessary. All this time we had spent shoulder to shoulder, and now, we faced the prospect of needing to go our separate ways, if only so our hunters had to find four separate targets rather than one group of four.

"Perhaps, as our hunters fall to us one by one and squad by squad, we'll cut off enough heads from the hydra that the body will die regardless," Argus surmised.

"Not exactly how hydras work, you know," Talon reminded.

"Maybe it's because nobody's cut off enough heads?"

"I'm pretty sure the whole point behind them is that you *can't.*"

"Yeah, well, good thing our enemy isn't an actual hydra. There are only so many bodies they can throw at us before they run out."

The Night Witch started to chuckle. "I think we'll be just fine, gentlemen. After all, we left the weakness of flesh behind."

"Who *was* it that coined that phrase between us, anyway?" I wondered aloud. Everyone then looked at me. "Oh."

Four directions. Four warriors. When the dawn came, we all had gone our separate ways, and the sirens were finally too distant to matter.

How much history would I now see that I'd left the insult of mortality behind?

How many skills would I now learn that I'd broken the chains the insult had bound me to?

I now had time to match my ambition, and so did three of my closest allies; I had no doubt I would live to see again.

When I first comprehended the weakness of my flesh... it disgusted me.

So I chose defiance.

AN INTERVIEW WITH GREGOR FJELLREV

WHEN DID YOU START WRITING AND WHY?

The main reason why that's a hard question is because it's hard to pinpoint exactly *when* I started writing in the form of stories. One could argue that's been happening since I learned how to write, as I was that kid in school who just spend all recess waving around a stick in some isolated corner, off in his own universe. It took until about high school before I was able to write anything novel-length, and only relatively recently was I able to start putting down the proper story of all those imaginary adventures in the form of the *Universal Defender* series. As for why... I never could learn how to draw. The written word was the next best thing.

WHICH AUTHORS OR BOOKS OR MEDIA INFLUENCED YOU THE MOST AS A WRITER?

With all the reading I had done throughout elementary and most of middle school, it's hard to pinpoint. When they say I was reading above my level, it mainly means that I was reading some hard stuff back then. I remember distinctly having to convince the librarian at Kilo middle school to let me check out *Prey.* Then there was the *Deptford Mice* trilogy, which belonged to that oddly high-populated category of rodents absolutely brutalizing each other in a fantasy setting. I also was quite a fan of the *Gregor the Overlander* series, so I suppose you could say that one, too.

WHICH AUTHORS OR BOOKS OR MEDIA HAD THE BIGGEST IMPACT ON YOU AS A PERSON?

Musashi's *Book of Five Rings* and his later *Dōkkodō* are solid candidates, along with the aforementioned *Gregor the Overlander* series.

WHICH OF YOUR ORIGINAL TWELVE PROMPT STORIES ARE YOU MOST PLEASED WITH?

That'd be tied between *Spheres of Annihilation* and *I Beheld Red Sparks.* The former was one that turned out far better than it had any right to, considering what madness was trying to tear my life to pieces back in February, and the latter was the more proper realization of a more surreal story I had hoped to achieve two months before, and was glad to be able to stick with it this time, rather than going back into my normal loop of gushing on about vengeance and retribution.

WHICH OF YOUR ORIGINAL TWELVE PROMPT STORIES DID YOU FIND THE MOST DIFFICULT TO WRITE?

That would go to *Avenger, Thyself Avenge.* It wouldn't stop raining, and I was going insane with hatred for rain. Couldn't bike to anywhere, internet wouldn't work because it was raining and I'm in the woods... it was a very annoying combination of having nothing to do, but the need to do *something.*

WHAT BOOK ON WRITING DO YOU RECOMMEND?

I'm not really one to recommend things, let alone how-to books. I can recommend *against* anything that excessively purports that one should 'write what they know'. Strict adherence to writing only what one knows is why there's so much literature about English professors considering adultery.

WHAT ADVICE WOULD YOU GIVE AN UNPUBLISHED WRITER?

I hate to give any cliché advice that one has heard a thousand times before from people half as qualified. The world is too full of non-advice that has all the helpfulness of a quote on a picture of a cat looking at a sunset, i.e., absolutely none. People want the credit of helping whilst not actually having to put forth the effort that meaningful contribution requires. Best advice I can give, then, is to regard the insipid cliché peddlers with the same validity one regards the opinions of a bible-touting cultist. Much as it is true that some clichés exist for a reason, that reason being that they work, it's not too difficult to instinctively tell the difference between that, and one of the mouth-breathing idiots who are exemplars of Churchill's quote 'the strongest argument against democracy is a five-minute conversation with the average voter.'

DO YOU HAVE A "DREAM PROJECT" AS A WRITER? WHAT WOULD IT BE?

That dream project already exists in the form of *Universal Defender*, but do not mistake this for me saying that it is fulfilled. There is still much to be done for that series, and the only dream I have nowadays is to commission the cover art for the next novella. It's fully finished at time of writing these answers, it just needs that cover art, but with my life continually refusing to improve, I can't spare the necessary funds to have the artwork done in the manner that I know it needs to be to do these characters justice.

YOUR STORIES ARE PUBLISHED IN THE SEASONAL *PROMPT* ANTHOLOGIES BUT ALSO AS A COLLECTION OF JUST YOUR OWN WORK. DID YOU HAVE A CONSCIOUS THEME FOR YOUR PERSONAL COLLECTION?

Conscious? Unlikely. Unconscious? Most likely, which graduated into consciousness as my pattern of retribution and self-avengement themes became clear.

YOU HAVE A BODY OF WORK OUTSIDE YOUR *PROMPT* STORIES. SHARE WHY THOSE OTHER WORKS ARE IMPORTANT TO YOU AND HOW THEY DIFFER FROM YOUR *PROMPT* STORIES.

Universal Defender is the flagship, the culmination of all the stories I was writing in my head, waiting for when I knew how better to put them in words, or at least more passably. The other novellas, *In Combat With Time*, *Talenostrum*, and *Night of the Whapwolf* are fun little experiments in style and theme, that I intend to expand on, if circumstances ever improve for me and I find myself with the spare energy. The will to create is heavily rationed for me, these days.

WHO DO YOU WRITE FOR AND HOW DOES IT DRIVE YOU TO CREATE?

I write what I would've liked to read about, and I also write for those who are tired of idiot plots. Spite drives me as more and more idiot plots keep getting published in all forms of media, and maybe one day, someone will notice that I'm actually bothering to write about competent characters putting forth all their effort and skill to solve problems.

OPTIMALLY, WE'RE ALWAYS GROWING AND IMPROVING AS AUTHORS. TALK ABOUT HOW YOU GREW OR CHANGED AS A WRITER OVER THE COURSE OF THE YEAR.

Well, I learned that story-a-month prompt writing isn't really for me. Nothing against the *Prompt* project, but I think my pathological dread of deadlines means that I'm not particularly cut out for it. I don't think I've ever even missed a deadline in my life, I just don't like 'em. I wouldn't say that I've grown as much as prevented regression in my ability, and the only major change has been in the fact that I've been rationing my creative ability as heavily as I have my sweat and money. I am glad to have been a part of this anthology, and I do not regret partaking in it in the slightest. That said, I probably wouldn't do it again.